KU-333-199

For Ellison

First published in the UK in 2022 by Nosy Crow Ltd
The Crow's Nest, 14 Baden Place,
Crosby Row, London SE1 1YW, UK

Nosy Crow Eireann Ltd
44 Orchard Grove, Kenmare
Co Kerry, V93 FY22, Ireland

Nosy Crow and associated logos are trademarks and/or registered
trademarks of Nosy Crow Ltd

Text © Dashe Roberts, 2022
Cover and chapter opener illustrations copyright © Bill Bragg, 2022

The right of Dashe Roberts to be identified as the author of this work
has been asserted.

All rights reserved

ISBN: 978 1 78800 893 8

A CIP catalogue record for this book is available from the British Library.

This book is sold subject to the condition that it shall not, by way of
trade or otherwise, be lent, hired out or otherwise circulated in any
form of binding or cover other than that in which it is published.
No part of this publication may be reproduced, stored in a retrieval
system, or transmitted in any form or by any means (electronic,
mechanical, photocopying, recording or otherwise) without the prior
written permission of Nosy Crow Ltd.

Printed and bound in Great Britain by Clays Ltd, Elcograf S.p.A.
Typeset by Tiger Media

Papers used by Nosy Crow are made from wood grown in
sustainable forests.

MIX
Paper from
responsible sources
FSC® C018072
www.fsc.org

1 3 5 7 9 10 8 6 4 2

www.nosycrow.com

CHAPTER 1

A Rocky Start

By the time we're finished digging, we'll have turned this whole valley inside out. Silas Sladan wiped his sweaty brow with a gloved hand, leaving a gritty streak across his face. "Fire in the hole!" he yelled, holding on to his safety helmet.

Behind him, a tight cluster of workers plugged their ears and braced themselves as he pulled the switch to the dynamite detonator.

PRAKOW! PRAKOW! PRAKOW! PRAKOW! PRAKOWWWWW! A series of thunderous explosions peppered the end of the mining tunnel in a fiery spiral. The rocky wall blasted apart, sending a gust of hot dust billowing down the long, tight corridor a quarter of a mile underground.

"Hooeey," shouted a tattooed miner with a ratty goatee. "That was a big 'un!"

"You said it, Riley." Relieved, Silas relaxed his tense muscles. *No cave-ins. No flooding. Nobody flattened by a falling boulder. I'd call that a success.*

Five months had passed since the Nu Co. pine sweetener factory was destroyed in a freak earthquake. The valley-shattering catastrophe had left many of Sticky Pines' residents unemployed, and revealed a startling discovery: massive rivers of thick, black goo flowed far below the region in enormous quantities. Baffling the local scientific community, the mysterious goo was identified as Nucralose – the sweet and highly valuable sap that seeped from the pines from which the town got its name. How tree sap could possibly be flowing underground, and where it was coming from, was a mystery that Nu Co.'s CEO, Mr Fisher, was determined to solve.

As soon as he'd learned of the subterranean goo, Fisher had set up a mining operation to collect the stuff day and night. Among several other former factory workers, Silas Sladan was retrained to join a special team tasked with uncovering the source of the Nucralose. Unfortunately, Silas was finding his new job to be dank, dreary and just plain dreadful.

When the soot from the blast finally settled, Silas removed his protective breathing mask and inhaled. The air smelled sweet. *That's a good sign.*

He unfurled a map on a folding table near the tunnel's entrance, showing the rivers of goo they'd discovered so far. They seemed to be more numerous closer to Black Hole Lake, so that's where he and his diggers were heading. But mining too close to the lake bed was a perilous operation.

"The explosions are the best part of this lame job," said a young man with a short Afro. He'd graduated from Sticky Pines High School just the year before, and he still had the acne to prove it. "Can I rig the dynamite next?"

"Sorry, Sam," Silas responded. "Your mom made me promise not to let you near any explosives. Wouldn't want you to lose any limbs, would we?"

Riley snorted as Sam flicked him on the arm.

A cage-like elevator descended into view, travelling down the smoky shaft leading to the surface. Packed with tired workers in grimy coveralls and dinged-up hard hats, the cage jolted to a stop on the mine floor.

A stout, soft-chinned man jostled past the other passengers to be first through the gated doors. His yellow helmet was so clean it was gleaming.

Silas greeted Fisher's second-in-command with a forced smile, the ends of his bushy black moustache turning up towards his dimples. "You smell that, Mr Murl?"

Murl closed his eyes. "The sweet stench of success." He clapped Silas on the shoulder.

"Good work, Sladan. With any luck, we'll locate the source of the goo in a matter of hours."

"About that." Silas rubbed his sore neck. "I was hoping to make it home for dinner tonight. Miranda's making *tamales* and my kids have been missing me lately."

"'Fraid I can't let you off early, Sladan." Murl shook his head. "Fisher's on a tight schedule. You understand."

Not really. Silas sighed. "You heard the man, *compadres*," he shouted at the crew disembarking from the elevator, their shovels and pickaxes in tow.

The clangs of metal against rock soon echoed through the tunnel, the seemingly endless day wearing on under the glare of artificial lights. *Just a little while longer*, Silas told himself for the zillionth time.

A pair of perspiring women trundled a cartful of rocks past him on their way to the disposal ramp. "Looks like we hit a cave system," said the taller of the two.

"Caves?" Silas's spirits lifted. *Sounds like we've found something interesting for once.* "Sam, Riley," he called.

He located them near the back of the tunnel, playing "hockey" with stones and sledgehammers. *Someone needs to teach those two some discipline.* Silas wished someone had talked some sense into him when he was their age, instead of letting him waste so much valuable time playing his guitar. *My father always said, there's no money in melodies.*

"We're going spelunking," he told the younger men.

"Sweet." Sam pumped his fist. He and Riley cheerfully followed Silas past the piles of debris, down to the rocky hole they'd just blasted open.

"Now, listen up," said Silas. "Caves can be very dangerous. You remember what I told you about mining this close to a big body of water?"

Sam raised his hand. "If we're not careful, we could accidentally bust through the lake bed."

"Which could have disastrous, even deadly,

consequences," Riley recited.

"That's right," said Silas. "We'll need to keep an eye out for cracks and leaks in the rock face. Once we've determined it's safe, we can continue the dig. You guys ready?"

"If I say no, can I go home?" said Riley.

"Just follow me," Silas grumbled as he led them into darkness.

The three men crouched low, sometimes crawling, as they made their way through the freshly exposed tunnel. Silas gagged as the sweet scent of Nucralose grew overpowering. Soon the narrow chasm they were probing yawned into an enormous cavern. Despite the workers' headlamps, it was difficult to make out much of their surroundings. Silas could hear a trickle of liquid coming from somewhere. *That had better not be water.*

"Hello," Sam shouted into the gloom. "Oh, oh, oh, oh, oh…" His deep voice echoed breezily around the void. "Your band should do a show down here, Mr Sladan. The acoustics are amazing."

"I don't want to discuss The Sticky Six," said Silas. He'd had to disband his beloved music group when he'd started his new job. He just didn't have enough time for hobbies any more. It was still a sore subject. "Can we get some light, please?"

Riley whipped out a flare and set it aflame with a SHGXXXSHH, bathing the cathedral-sized cave in flickering orange hues.

Silas's breath escaped all at once. *What on the round blue Earth…* A thick river of Nucralose, as black as night, slowly gurgled along the side of the domed cavern. Above it, sinewy twists of wood branched like exposed blood vessels down the jagged wall, straight into the sticky goo.

"Are those tree roots?" asked Sam, agog.

"This far underground?" scoffed Silas. "We're more than four hundred feet below the surface. Don't be stupid."

"No, I think he's right," said Riley. He sauntered closer, shining his headlamp at the woody protrusions. "I reckon these are sticky pine roots. Think they're sucking up the sap from all the way down here?"

"Like a bunch of silly straws?" Sam nodded. "Yeah, that makes sense."

Silas smacked his forehead. "My wife taught you both middle school science. You know very well that's not how trees work."

"Maybe sticky pines aren't normal trees," Riley ventured.

"And maybe that stuff's not sap," said Sam.

The hair on the back of Silas's neck stood to attention. *What else could it be?* He shook his head to fend off an impending headache. "Let's get to work and make sure this cave is safe. Riley, check the right side. Sam, head towards the back."

The three men split up, weaving carefully through the dim cavern, their headlamps casting looming shadows across a landscape strewn with towering stalagmites and mounds of rubble knocked loose from the explosion.

Silas shone his headlamp up along the impossible tree roots until they disappeared into the cave ceiling. He narrowed his eyes as he spotted strange shapes carved into the rock high above. *What the...* The dome was covered in time-worn depictions of creatures big and small, all of which had been etched into the stone centuries ago. Some were normal woodland animals, but others looked like they'd been ripped out of old legends. A snake with nine heads, a wolf with curved fangs, a creature with the body of a man and the head and legs of a bison, and many more.

"Monsters." Silas shivered.

"What'd you find?" asked Riley. He directed his torch up towards the centre of the ceiling, highlighting a colossal figure: a dragon with a scaly, moustachioed snout and eagle-like talons on its hands and feet. Its winged, dog-like physique curled around an enormous orb.

"Cool." Riley scratched his patchy beard. "How'd prehistoric hillbillies carve that junk all the way up there?"

"Beats me," said Silas.

"Hey," Sam called from the far side of the cavern. "Look over here."

Cripes. What now?

Silas jogged round a wide pillar of rock, then shone his torch towards the back of the cave. Sam was standing fifty metres away, pointing at a trickling waterfall of viscous goo that oozed out of the ceiling and ran down the back wall like syrup down a stack of pancakes. The gloopy substance dribbled down jagged stones, pooling in nooks and crannies before it spilled into the thick river flowing below.

Riley whistled. "Well, I guess we know what's feedin' that crick."

"Could the source of all the Nucralose be just behind this wall?" Sam rubbed his hands together excitedly.

Silas's pulse quickened with hope. "Let's not jump to conclusions." He tried and failed to hide his delight. *I'll definitely be getting a bonus for this.*

"Let's blast through the goo-fall now," said Riley. "I'll go and get the dynamite. BING, BANG,

BOOM, we finish the job and we can get back above ground and see some daylight for once."

"We can't just blast through." Silas knocked on Riley's helmet. "You want the whole lake to crash down on us?"

"Hey, guys," Sam called out. He'd found a cove off to the right, hidden behind a group of lumpy stalagmites. "I found some more carvings."

Silas and Riley hustled over, their tools jangling on their belts. Riley set his flare down to light the shallow tunnel. Inside was a shiny black onyx slab the size and shape of a door. At chest height, someone had engraved a large circle surrounded by squiggly lines. *Looks like a kid's drawing of the sun.* Silas peered closer, noticing that the lines were made up of many small holes, each big enough to fit the tip of a pencil. There was a series of strange symbols inside the sun, all encircling a thumb-sized white stone embedded in its centre.

Sam leaned in. "That looks like a button."
Silas pulled him back. "Don't touch it."

"Why not?"

"You don't know what it does."

Riley jostled between them. "So what? I bet nothing would happen. I say we push it."

"Do not do that," ordered Silas.

"Oh, come on," Sam laughed. "We're only human. You see a mysterious button, you gotta push it, right?"

Silas pinched the bridge of his nose. "OK, boys, we're heading back to the tunnel right now, and we're going to report all of this to—"

Before he could finish, Riley reached out and punched the button with the side of his fist. There was a CLICK, as if some unseen gear had shifted.

Silas's throat tightened. "What did you just do?"

All three men fell silent, waiting. Nothing happened.

"See?" said Riley. "I told you it wouldn't—"

GKSSSSSSSSSSSSSSSSHHHHHHHHH.

A mist of glittering black dust blew out of the carved holes, engulfing Silas, Riley and Sam in a shimmering cloud. The three men doubled over, coughing.

"What is this stuff?" Sam wheezed.

"I don't know," Silas sputtered. It felt like dozens of tiny fingers were tickling the inside of his lungs. He might have laughed if he weren't so terrified. "Let's get out of here," he cried, his head spinning. He ran, accidentally kicking Riley's flare and sending it careening into the river, where it was extinguished.

Guided only by the jiggling lights attached to their helmets, the disoriented miners stumbled towards the tunnel entrance, tripping over loose stones, their own feet and each other. When they finally reached the blast hole, Silas shoved the other two in first, then tumbled after them. One by one, gasping, they spilled out the other side.

Silas collapsed by a pile of gravel, taking slow, juddering breaths until the tickling sensation subsided. After several minutes, his coughing eased and his heart slowed. He looked up to find a short, auburn-haired worker named Carleen with dirt-smudged cheeks peering down at him. The unlit lamp on her helmet mirrored back his own face. His normally brown irises were emitting bright-green light, like starry emeralds.

Whoa.

"Hot jeepers," Carleen yelped. "What's the matter with your peepers?"

Dazed, Silas rubbed his eyelids with the heels of his palms, then blinked blearily at the half-dozen workers watching him from afar.

"Wait." Carleen leaned in closer, chuckling nervously. "Sorry, Sy, for a minute there I could've sworn your eyes were *glowing*." She shuddered. "Maybe I've been down here too long." She helped him to his feet.

Sam and Riley were across the tunnel, still coughing. Two burly workers pounded on their backs until they were once again breathing freely.

"What happened back there?" asked Carleen.

Silas screwed up his face as he tried to remember, but everything seemed fuzzy. In a rush, his head cleared, leaving a sensation of pure joy. He, Sam and Riley turned to one another and began giggling uncontrollably.

"What's the joke?" said one of the burly miners.

Silas grinned like a golden retriever. "Listen up." He cleared his throat, attempting to put on a serious tone. "Those caves are not safe," he announced. "There are ... water leaks! And cracks. Cracks allllll over the place."

Riley smirked and Sam nodded earnestly.

Carleen threw her helmet on the ground. "You mean all this digging's been for nothing?"

"I guess so." Silas shrugged. "Tell you what – why don't we all take the rest of the day off?"

Riley clapped. "That's a wicked idea."

"You, uh, sure we can do that, Sy?" Carleen perked up.

"I'll let the bossman know we can't possibly dig through such a dangerous cavity." Silas nudged his way through the throng of pleasantly surprised miners, none of whom seemed likely to complain.

Carleen stopped him with a hand on his shoulder. "Are you sure you're feeling all right?"

A serene smile graced Silas's face. "Oh, yes." He took a deep breath and let it out with a satisfying whoosh. "I've never felt better in my life."

CHAPTER 2

Code Conspirators

"You are wrong, Gertie!" Tex Arkhipov threw his pencil down on the faded blue carpet.

"I'm right." Gertie Lee tossed her black bob. "You know I'm right, and so does everyone else." She searched the sunny school computer room for a consensus from the other newsies, but everyone was averting their eyes.

Tex and Gertie act like such dinguses these days, thought Lucy Sladan. She was slouched at a computer at the back of the room browsing websites about the paranormal instead of working on the Sticky Pines Elementary and Middle School (SPEAMS) newspaper.

"Fart jokes are not lowbrow," Tex insisted. He swung a long leg over the back of a plastic chair and sat. "A fart is a universally humorous biological function," he explained, smoothing his grey button-up shirt. "It ties all humanity together in one big, weird family. A band of beggars, the kings and queens of England. Farters, all of them."

"Some more than others," said Lucy.

Gertie marched over to the whiteboard, wrote the word "FART" and drew an X through it. "Tex, your article is about the ecological calamity unfolding in the Big Crater Valley. A quarter of the wildlife in the area has disappeared and nobody is paying any attention." Gertie was fuming now. "The bat population alone is down fifty-three per cent. It's an Ecotastrophe. It's an Ecopocalypse—"

"It's an Econvenient Truth?" offered Smitty, a girl with mousy hair and round glasses who followed Gertie around like an eager puppy.

"Ooh." Gertie brightened. "Now, that's a headline."

The "newsies" club had recently received an upgrade after Mr Fisher made a generous donation to the school. It was part of his bid to improve Nu Co.'s local reputation after a series of disasters involving the shadowy company. Since Fisher's son Milo was a member, the *SPEAMS Sentinel* newspaper had moved out of the basement boiler room and was now being retooled to exist entirely online.

Chewing on a lock of wavy purple hair, Lucy scribbled a note and passed it under the table to Milo.

The slight, fine-featured young man stopped working on the photo of the volleyball club he was editing. He unfolded the note and read the strange symbols Lucy had drawn.

Over the last few months, Lucy and Milo had memorised the compendium of shapes, dots and swirly lines that formed the pictorial language of the Pretenders: a race of shapeshifters they'd discovered who'd been living secretly in Sticky Pines for generations. Though some of the creatures disguised themselves as people, it had recently been revealed that many more of them took the shape of animals.

Lucy and Milo suspected that the recent decline in the wildlife population was due to the fact that all of the Pretenders were in hiding after a brutal confrontation with Mr Fisher's forces. After Nu Co.'s private security team had cornered a group of them, scores of animals in the valley had revealed themselves to be their shapeshifting brethren. Combining their efforts, the creatures had used their awesome extranatural powers to rip open the ground beneath the Nu Co. factory, swallowing the iconic building whole. Mr Fisher had almost fallen into the chasm, but Milo and Lucy had managed to pull him back from the brink.

Lucy had tried to explain the incredible story to Gertie, but the super-serious school news editor hadn't believed her. *So much for the power of the press.*

Milo decoded Lucy's note and stifled a snort. He retrieved a pen from his polo shirt pocket, jotted something down on the reverse side of the paper and passed it back to his friend.

Lucy read: "Tex should not be chicken. He should asking Gertie to spring dance. She sure say yes!"

They hadn't quite gotten the hang of the Pretenders' language yet.

Lucy cleaned her glasses on her yellow flannel shirt. *Are you kidding me? Gertie'd never go to the Spring Fling with Tex. She's a NINTH-GRADER with a nose ring, and he's a seventh-grader who washes his jeans roughly once a year.* She scrawled a response in the margins: "Fish, your head is full of nuts."

Milo had initially been reluctant to memorise the shifters' symbols. He still seemed upset about what had happened between them and his father. *Even though it was Fisher's fault for attacking them in the first place.* But once Lucy had suggested that the glyphs could be used as a secret way to discuss the brain-busting supernatural activity they'd uncovered, he'd come on board with the idea.

Unfortunately, none of the human Pretenders had resurfaced, and Lucy's investigation into the origin of their species had been cold for months. Mandy Millepoids had shuttered his beloved downtown candy shop. Alastair Chelon had supposedly moved to Canada to work as a lumberjack. Meanwhile, Carlos Felina had allegedly joined Marietta and Kenzo Corbin at a spiritual retreat in the Himalayas. And word was that "Scruffy" Steve Kozlowski, Silas's bandmate in The Sticky Six, was "backpacking across South America to seek musical nirvana".

Most cheekily of all, the local newspaper had announced that the Strickses had moved to Hawaii after winning the scratch-card lottery. *The monkey-sniffing lottery.* Lucy was especially disappointed that her own parents had fallen for that one. *Adults will believe anything these days.*

The donkier the better.

As for Thingus, the young shapeshifter who'd befriended Milo and Lucy before the terrifying events that had unfolded at the factory last autumn, he'd simply disappeared without a trace. Lucy hoped he was OK. Milo never seemed to want to talk about him.

Milo read Lucy's latest note and cracked up. Before he could write a response, a hand reached down from behind him and snatched it out of his startled grasp.

"Working hard, I see?" Principal Pakuna's long face was drawn into a frown as she read the incomprehensible note. "What's this supposed to mean?"

Lucy uncrossed her hiking boots and sat up straight. "It's just a few harmless doodles, Principal P."

Pakuna grunted and slipped the note into the pocket of the orange corduroys she may well have been wearing since nineteen seventy-five. "Ms Lee," she said, glaring at the word "FART" on the whiteboard, "you assured me this club would not waste valuable school resources."

Gertie jumped to her feet. "Principal Pakuna, I can assure you we're working as hard as a quartz quarry over here. Smitty!" She snapped her fingers.

The small girl sprang up from her seat to erase the contents of the whiteboard.

"The *Sentinel* app and website go live at the end of the week," said Pakuna. "Parents, teachers and students alike will be using it. The school board is breathing down my neck to ensure the launch runs smoothly, so we're relying on you, Ms Lee. Are you sure you don't require any," she glanced at Lucy and Milo, "supervision?"

"Everything is under control," Gertie assured her. "Please, allow me to show you our latest innovation." She straightened her turquoise blazer and headed for Lucy's desk.

Lucy scrambled to close twelve browser tabs about a UFO sighting in Arizona and brought up the *Sentinel* site. The banner read: **THE SPEAMS SENTINEL: BROUGHT TO YOU BY NU CO.**

Pakuna leaned in to review Lucy's monitor, her long hair draped over her shoulder like a silver curtain.

Dutifully, Lucy clicked on Nu Co.'s creepy grinning clown mascot, popping up a window with some text-based links and lots of empty space.

"It is called 'SPEAMS Memes'," announced Tex. He strode over from his desk by the window.

"It's a message board?" Principal Pakuna asked flatly.

"It is a digital marketplace of ideas," said Tex, hands aloft, "where students can coordinate study groups, exchange views on cultural events, praise their teachers—"

"Invite each other to school dances," Milo added with a knowing wink.

Tex blushed. "Toli and I designed it together." He nodded towards his younger brother, a fifth-grader who was seated at the front of the room.

Toli, the paper's resident music critic, was off in his own little world, his blond hair swept rakishly over one eye, a pair of old-school headphones over his ears.

Tex clapped to get his attention.

Toli peeled off his headphones, filling the lab with the muffled thump of trance beats. "Huh?" he said, as if awakening to the fact that there were other people in the room.

"The message board?" said Tex.

Toli drummed exuberantly on the table. "SPEAMS Memes will be as epic as Thelonius Monk teaming up with John Coltrane in the East Village. It's going to launch the *Sentinel* into the stratosphere." With a thumbs-up, he snapped his headphones back on, bobbed his head and went back to typing up his latest album review.

Pakuna glowered at Gertie. "I said no social media."

"Because of trolls and bullying." Gertie nodded solemnly. "Very wise. Which is why we have *her*." She jerked her thumb at Lucy.

Lucy waved, feebly. "Hello. I'm your friendly neighbourhood moderator."

"Her?" said the principal.

Me. After writing one too many stories about conspiracies and the supernatural (*it was ONLY ONE and it was nothing but the PLURPING TRUTH!*), Lucy's article ideas were no longer welcome at the *Sentinel*. Instead, her role was to scour the new message board and ban all manner of online trolls. Toli had warned her that the job could cause lasting psychological damage, which was enough promise of excitement for Lucy to accept the position.

"I'll be checking in on you tomorrow," the principal said before she exited and disappeared down the echoey school hallway.

Gertie clapped to get everyone's attention. "OK, people, you heard her. It's time to get your boots in gear."

The computer room filled with the demented clacking of fifteen sets of fingers typing madly.

"Speaking of billboards..." Lucy whispered

to Milo.

He peeked round his monitor. "Your doohickey is finished? Already?"

Lucy patted the dusty backpack hanging off her chair, eliciting a metallic clank. "I stayed up late last night fiddling with the wires. You still down to help me set it up?"

"Sladan," Gertie barked. "Stop distracting the Photo Editing Department."

Lucy slumped in her seat. "Why'm I always the one who gets in trouble?"

"Well," Milo smirked, "you do tend to stand out from the crowd. I'll be there." He went back to editing photos.

Lucy checked the time on her computer. *Only half an hour to go.* She bounced her knees excitedly under the table. *And we'll finally track down those missing Pretenders, once and for all.*

CHAPTER 3

Up and
Away

CRACK! Milo snapped the maple branch he had lifted so Lucy could pass through the underbrush.

"Whoops," he apologised. *So much for chivalry.*

"Let's try to keep the forest intact, shall we?" said Lucy. She ducked under the broken limb, which was festooned with fresh star-shaped leaves.

The thirteen-year-old friends tromped through the lush woodland, passing through groves of twisted sticky pine trees dripping with black sap, the crunchy ground covered with green and purple ferns that fanned out like peacocks. Lucy paused to pluck a handful of stinky yellow blooms from a patch of skunk cabbage, tossing them at Milo until he chased her all the way down to the banks of the Ungula River.

Red-faced and breathless, Lucy took off her socks and boots and rolled up the tattered hems of her jeans as she prepared to cross the waterway. Milo sat beside her and did the same, rolling his khakis above his knees. He dipped a toe in the icy river, its banks swollen with snow run-off, then retrieved a pair of water shoes from his backpack and slipped them on his bare feet.

"You're so prepared," said Lucy.

"It pays to stay on your toes in Sticky Pines. You never know when you may need to outrun a trout that's really an ancient sea monster."

"Pretenders are aliens, not monsters," said Lucy. "And they're more scared of us than we are of them."

That's easy for you to say. They didn't nearly

toss your father down a bottomless pit last autumn.
"Why are you so sure they're aliens?"

"It's called 'gut instinct'." Lucy tied her shoelaces together and slung her boots over her shoulder. "All the best paranormal investigators trust it more than anything else."

"Yeah, they would." Milo couldn't help but admire her undaunted certainty.

Secretly he hoped the shapeshifters were gone for good, whatever they were. He'd seen what they could do with their electrical powers and morphing abilities. They could hide anywhere undetected, travel through lightning and even change the weather. They were terrifying. For Milo, the fact that both his father and his best friend were actively *chasing* these creatures was baffling beyond belief.

But if they really did disappear forever, would Lucy still want to hang out with me? And would Dad still want to live in Sticky Pines? It wasn't the first time he'd asked himself these questions.

The trees swayed in the breeze, leaves rustling gently. Milo listened quietly until his reverie was interrupted by Lucy sloshing into the river.

"Come on," she called.

They were halfway across, picking their way over some mossy stones, when Milo saw something move in the bushes on the other bank. *No, not something. Some*one. Whoever it was appeared to be wearing camouflage. Milo nearly lost his balance on the slippery terrain.

"Whoa." Lucy caught him by the arm. "You OK?"

"There's someone over there." He pointed.

Lucy scanned the riverbank. "I don't see anyone," she said. "Are you sure?"

But Milo couldn't make out the human shape he'd seen before. Now there was nothing but bark and bushes. "No." He looked around. "But I really feel like we're being watched."

Lucy squinted up towards the clouds. "I don't see any Nu Co. drones." She patted Milo's arm. "Your dad uses high-tech surveillance to make sure you tie your shoes; it's no wonder you're paranoid."

"Just because I'm paranoid doesn't mean nothing's out to get us."

Lucy shrugged, then tromped on.

Their destination loomed on the horizon: a monumental billboard towering over the forest canopy, overlooking Black Hole Lake. The imposing advertisement featured the Nu Co. clown, its red-painted mouth smiling wide. The jovial corporate jester was wearing a hard hat with a shining headlamp illuminating the new tagline: "Nu Co. – Solutions for a Safer World". At the top of the frame was a rainbow overlaid with the company's most popular products: packets of sap sweetener, a bucket of industrial-strength pine glue, a box of organic bandages and a can of Nu Co. Cola. Missing, Milo noted, were any of the brightly coloured substances his father's corporation used as biological weapons against the town's supernatural residents. *It's probably best not to advertise that part of the company's mission, for the time being.*

Milo had gathered that Nu Co. was working on a top-secret new formula, but it was so classified that his father refused to tell him anything about it. Which was fine with Milo. Lucy never stopped plumbing him for details about his dad's endeavours, and the last thing he wanted to do was lie to her.

When they reached the base of the billboard, Milo blanched as he took in the height of the thing.

"Do we really need to put your UFO detector all the way up there?"

"The higher it goes, the better," said Lucy. "Mind if I head up first?"

With a running start, Lucy jumped and caught the lowest rung on the ladder at the back of the pole. Milo rushed over to help bolster her kicking feet. Her backpack hanging heavily on her shoulders, she hoisted herself up and scurried skyward. Giving himself a quick pep talk, Milo leapt up behind her, braced himself against his fear of heights and climbed.

They scaled the billboard without stopping, their sweaty hands clanging steadily against the rungs. CLONG, CLONG, CLONG. *It's amazing how efficiently you can move when the alternative is plummeting to your death.* The ladder ended at a wooden platform with a metal railing situated beneath the giant advertisement.

"Wow," Milo whispered as he climbed on to the wooden planks and took in the view.

The sun was setting behind the Dentalia Mountains, which encircled the verdant borders of the Big Crater Valley like a snow-capped crown. Below, Black Hole Lake glinted in the evening sun, its misty waters dotted with the white froth of motorboats and a few swimmers near the shore.

"I haven't seen this much of Sticky Pines since that day at the fair," said Lucy, leaning on the railing. "Do you remember when we rode the Ferris wheel?"

Of course I remember.

"Careful," he warned. "Don't get too close to the edge." He still had nightmares about his father's near-death experience.

Lucy opened her pack and pulled out a football-sized cylinder with solar panels and four telescopic antennae, which she carefully arranged. Next, she placed a curved metal dish against one side and screwed it in.

Milo scrunched his nose. "That thing looks ... complicated."

"It's just a receiver that picks up elecro-magnetic waves from space," Lucy explained. "My mom helped design it."

"You think it'll really detect messages from UFOs?"

"I *know* it will," said Lucy. She gazed up at the sky. "The Pretenders' ship has gotta be hiding up there somewhere, and this baby," she smacked the detector, "is gonna get me the proof I need."

Milo considered tossing the contraption over the edge and making it look like an accident, but instead he helped Lucy attach it to the railing with a set of Velcro straps. When it seemed secure, she pressed a button on the side. A small green indicator lit up.

Finished with their task, the kids sat for a spell, dangling their legs over the side of the platform. Milo peered over the edge and a rush of vertigo fluttered through his belly. He quickly focused on the sunset, the clouds slowly turning pink.

"What if the Pretenders aren't aliens?" he asked.

Lucy tossed her hair over her shoulder, in accordance with the breeze. "What else could they possibly be?"

"Fairies, witches, vengeful gods…" said Milo.

"You think they're *gods*?" Lucy guffawed. "I'll bet Mrs Stricks would get a kick out of that."

"All we know is that they've been here for a very long time," he said. "Maybe they're an undiscovered species that evolved on Earth? Like vampires."

"Vampires aren't a species. And how many other creatures on this planet can shoot lightning out of their fingers?"

"Ever heard of electric eels?"

Lucy scowled. "Besides them."

A set of lights at the base of the billboard flickered on and lit up the ad behind them.

Lucy sneered at the colossal clown. "I should've brought some spray paint to give that thing a moustache. I wish you knew more about what Nu Co. was up to these days. My dad says they've been harvesting enough Nucralose to fill a hundred Olympic-sized swimming pools."

"I've been meaning to ask you," said Milo, hoping to change the subject from his father's business affairs to a more pressing matter, "are you going to the school dance?" As soon as he'd asked the question, his mouth snapped shut. *There, I finally said it.*

"I dunno," said Lucy. "It's probably going to be lame. Have you ever been to a dance?"

"I've been to a gala. Does that count?"

"No." Lucy made a face.

"Are you planning on going with anyone?"

asked Milo.

"To the dance?" said Lucy, perplexed. "I guess I figured that if I go, I'd just hang out with you and Tex and we'd make fun of everyone's outfits."

Milo rested his chin on the cool metal balustrade. "The thing is," he said, mustering some courage, "if Tex is going to ask Gertie to go with him—"

"That won't happen," said Lucy.

"But what if he does and she says yes? Then what?"

"Then it'd be just me and you making fun of people, wouldn't it?"

"Seems that way," said Milo. He stared down at his knees. *I can't believe I'm actually going to do this.* "So, um, if that's the case, then, um, why don't we just go ahead and make it offic–"

SKREE! SKREE SKREE SKREE! He was interrupted by the frenzied cries of dozens of bats as a cloud of the creatures flapped chaotically over the billboard, close enough that the kids could feel the beat of their leathery black wings. Milo ducked and shielded his hair while Lucy, ever the contrarian, jumped to her feet.

ZZZZZOOP, ZZZZZOOOOP. Following close behind the squeaking creatures was a pair of sleek silver drones, darting back and forth in an attempt to corral them.

"They're after the bats," Lucy shouted.

The drones chased the cloud of flying mammals in a zigzag pattern, successfully splitting one away from the rest of the group. One of the remote robots fired a net, which unspooled in the air, just missing the animal.

Lucy gasped. "They almost got one!"

The rest of the bats swirled defensively, diving at the net-spitting drone as their targeted comrade tried to fly away. The second drone swooped up from below and sprayed a stream of yellow gas that enveloped the zigzagging creature. Oddly, the lone bat slowed and began to fly slowly in a circle.

"What is that stuff?" said Lucy.

An acrid, overly sweet stench filled the air as the yellow substance drifted towards them on the breeze. Milo knew exactly what it was. *Engineered Nucralose. That must be Dad's newest technological breakthrough.*

A shriek of horror rang out from the other bats and they redoubled their attack, diving and clawing at the drone's propellers until it began smoking and spitting sparks.

Those aren't real bats. Milo shrank back. *They're shifters.*

With a ZRRRRUM, a third drone whizzed heroically over the billboard and joined the other two, scattering the attacking animals. The first drone puttered back to the bat that was flying in circles and fired another net, this time entangling it.

Dodging and darting, the other creatures regrouped and formed a neat V. In one collective movement, they dived down towards Black Hole Lake. Lucy squealed with alarm as the bats plunged straight into the murky, misty water.

They never resurfaced.

The drones hovered for a few moments, then zipped back towards the Nu Co. property, carrying the stupefied shapeshifter with them.

"What the greasefire did we just witness?" said Lucy, already rifling through her backpack for her notebook. "Those bats were Pretenders, right? And what was that crazy yellow gas?" She crouched down and started scribbling. "This is why the animal population has dropped so much in Sticky Pines. Nu Co.'s been hunting and capturing shapeshifters one by one. If Gertie Lee had any idea of what was actually going on round here…" Lucy looked up at Milo. "What does your dad plan to do with the bat?"

"I honestly have no idea," said Milo, kicking his feet in the air. It was mostly true. Though he didn't know exactly what his father was up to, he knew enough to be sure that he had a plan. *Someday soon, Dad's going to track down every one of the Pretenders, and save this whole valley in the process.*

CHAPTER 4

Out of
Tune

DUNG CHIGA-CHIGA-CHIGA DUNG CHIGA-CHIGA-CHIGA DUNG DUNG DUNG! *Whose music is that?* Yawning, Lucy peeled her eyelids open. It sounded like a squadron of pelicans having a beak fight in an oil-barrel factory. *Ugh. I never get to sleep in on Saturdays.*

Kicking her half-finished maths homework out of the way, she shuffled across her bedroom floor, rescued a pair of relatively clean jeans from the laundry basket and followed the sizzling scent of spices down the creaky attic stairs of the Sladan household.

When she reached the kitchen, she found her father dancing in front of the stove in sweatpants and the holey AC/DC T-shirt he wore when he was fixing things in the garage. Silas tossed the egg he was frying in the air, spun around and caught it in the pan. Errol, the family wolfhound, sat by the oven with his tongue hanging out the side of his mouth.

Dad sure seems upbeat today.

"Welcome to the party, Lucita," said Lucy's mother.

Miranda Sladan was seated at the kitchen island, sipping from a steaming mug emblazoned with the words "#1 Teacher". Behind her, Lucy's little sister Willow was laying on the living room rug watching cartoons.

"How ya doin, squiddo?" Silas turned down the Iron Maiden blasting from the stereo. "Did I wake you?"

Lucy pouted.

Silas stirred a pot of bubbling tomato sauce that smelled like seven kinds of heaven. Errol barked, demanding a taste.

"*Huevos rancheros* are not for dogs, buddy," Silas scolded.

Lucy rubbed her eyes and took a seat on the stool next to her mother. "Is it somebody's birthday?"

"Nope." Miranda gazed at her husband with tired curiosity. "Your father's just decided to treat us this morning."

"Anything for you, my magnificent goddess." Silas winked.

"Gross," said Lucy.

"Food's ready," he called, scooping the salsa over a tray of crisp tortillas topped with beans and fried eggs. "Luce, set the table, please. I have an important announcement to make."

Yawning, Miranda refilled her coffee. "An announcement?" she said. "This is the first I've heard of it."

"That's why it's called an *announcement*, Mom," said Willow. She moved a pile of folded laundry from the table to the couch, then took a seat.

At Silas's insistence, they ate breakfast first, talking and joking in a way they hadn't done in ages. Lucy's father seemed happier than she'd seen him since he'd started his new job. *Did he get a promotion? Are we getting another dog? Or a swimming pool?*

"All right," said Miranda, when everyone had finished eating. She looked expectantly at Silas. "We've waited long enough."

Willow set her near-empty plate on the floor, where Errol was waiting patiently. He licked it clean in a matter of seconds.

Silas pressed his lips tightly against a smile so big Lucy thought he might burst.

"Oh, just tell us, for cripes' sake," she said.

Silas took a dramatic pause. "We are all moving to Los Angeles, California!" He beamed.

"What?" said Miranda. "You're joking, right?"

"Did you put crazy pills in the salsa?" Lucy seconded.

"Where's California?" asked Willow.

Silas clapped his hands. "It's down south," he said. "It's warm and sunny, and it's filled with artists and actors and musicians. And there are beaches. Looooots of beaches."

"I like the beach." Willow was clearly warming to the idea.

"But my whole life is here," said Lucy. A lump rose in her throat. She'd lived in Sticky Pines since she was born. The town contained everything that made life amazing. Her friends, her school, the undeniable proof of extranatural oddities...

Miranda scooted her chair out so fast Errol had to jump out of the way. She stood, a vein at her temple bulging. "We're not moving anywhere."

"Oh, but honey," said Silas.

Lucy noticed that her father was still smiling despite the barely suppressed fury in her mother's voice. *Not smart, Dad.*

"Think of all the fun we'd have," he continued obliviously. "We could get a convertible and drive around with the top down." He cha-cha'd over to Miranda's side of the table and tried to engage her in a dance. She stiffened.

Dude. Lucy and Willow exchanged a look that meant "Mom's about to blow a mega-gasket". The sisters retreated behind the coffee table, where Willow threw her arms around Errol and pulled him close.

"Silas," said Miranda, clearly searching for the appropriate words to use next. "Can you explain to me EXACTLY why you want us to quit our jobs, uproot our family and move to *the beach*?"

Wide-eyed, like a baby deer unaware that the mountain lion in front of it was not interested in developing a meaningful relationship, Silas trotted into the living room and retrieved his acoustic guitar. "Let me show you." He slipped the strap around his shoulder and started rocking out to an unfamiliar, atonal, head-banging tune.

Lucy recoiled. *He can't be serious.*

Miranda placed her hand on Silas's guitar strings, blocking his frenzied strumming. "What. Is. That?" she asked.

"It's a new song I wrote," said Silas. "I call it 'Raven-Haired Love Mermaid'. It's inspired by you, sweetie."

Lucy's jaw dropped. Willow theatrically crossed herself.

"Am I to understand," said Miranda, the tension in her voice reaching a peak, "that you want us all to move to California so you can pursue a career in MUSIC?"

"Yeah." Silas grinned. "I'm starting a new band with a couple of guys from the mine."

"Please tell me you're not referring to the teenagers you told me about yesterday."

"Riley is twenty-three," he corrected her.

"SILAS ELIJAH SLADAN," Miranda yelled.

Whoa. Mom's in middle-name territory.

"You are thirty-nine years old," said Miranda. "You can't uproot your family and move them to LA so you can chase a pipe dream about becoming a middle-aged rock star."

"Why not?"

"Because you *can't*."

"Says who? You're not my mom."

Lucy felt like she was witnessing a tennis match where the fuzzy yellow ball had been replaced with a hand grenade.

"Girls," said Miranda, not even looking at her daughters. "GO UPSTAIRS."

Lucy grabbed Willow by the elbow and Errol by the collar and herded them down the hallway, up the rickety staircase and into her attic bedroom. Even with the door shut, they could hear shouting.

"What the hot snot was that about?" asked Lucy.

Willow sat cross-legged in her sister's bright orange beanbag chair, looking more amused than concerned. "Dad's probably just playing a prank on us. Remember when he put a fake spider in Mom's soup?"

Lucy threw herself on to her rumpled bed, where Errol had found a comfortable nook, and stared up at the slanted timber ceiling. "I don't think so, Will. Dad's acting especially weird."

Willow drew her knees up to her chest. "What do you think's wrong with him?"

"Maybe something happened to him at the Nu Co. mine. He came home early on Monday, didn't he?"

"Yeah."

"Did he say why?"

Willow shook her head, tying her pink hoodie strings into a makeshift moustache.

Lucy hurried over to the laptop on her desk and booted up her messaging app. "I wonder if Mr Fisher has something to do with this."

"Oof." Willow collapsed on the beanbag. "Ever since the Fishers moved out here, everything's gone crazypants. Why is Milo's dad such a dishrag?"

"Beats me," said Lucy. "At least Fish is a good guy."

"I wish *they'd* move to Los Angeles." Willow tiptoed across the room and placed her ear against the door. "I think they're done yelling.

I'm gonna go see if there's any more beans."

As her sister headed downstairs with Errol bounding at her heels, Lucy finished typing her message:

Fish, have you heard of anything strange going on at the Nu Co. mines? My dad's acting bonko and I have a bad feeling something happened to him at work. Could you maybe find out if your dad knows anything about it? Pretty please?

Lucy hesitated before sending the message. It had been a while since Milo had shared any major info about what his father was up to. *Why is that? Could he be keeping things from me?* But surely, she reasoned, after everything they'd experienced together, he wouldn't hold back any important information from her now. *Fish is my friend. He's on my side. I know he is.*

She hit send.

CHAPTER 5

Balls in
the Air

KNOCK, KNOCK.

"You may enter," came Mr Fisher's deep voice from behind the heavy closed doors.

Milo entered his father's office on the second floor of the spacious family lodge. The pine-panelled room overlooked his stepmother Kaitlyn's freshly planted pastel rose garden.

"Do you have a minute?" asked Milo. He'd just received a worrying message from Lucy about her dad's strange behaviour. Despite some misgivings, he'd promised her he'd find out what he could.

"For you, kiddo? Sure." Mr Fisher looked up

from the map spread across his desk that featured dark, wavy lines branching out in a circle around Black Hole Lake. "I was just going over the plan for the latest dig." Fisher rolled his Scandinavian leather chair back from the desk and beckoned his son to enter.

Milo strolled in, glancing at a photo of himself smiling proudly in a cap and gown the day he graduated from kindergarten. "Do you think you could help me with my golf swing? I'd like to try out for the school team."

"Your swing, eh?" Mr Fisher sat up in his chair. "I don't know. I do have a lot of work to do."

"It's Saturday," said Milo. "And you deserve a break."

Fisher glanced uneasily out of the window. Lately, he'd been wary of spending too much time outdoors, now he knew that a frightening amount of the wildlife in the Big Crater Valley consisted of bizarre shapeshifting freaks. Before he'd ramped up his efforts to hunt the creatures down, every car he owned had been routinely covered in drippy splats of bird poop.

Milo pressed him before he had a chance to say no. "I've already set up the equipment on the back lawn."

Fisher chuckled. "Far be it from me to discourage my only son from taking the initiative."

He followed Milo through the lodge's white hallways adorned with sparse, abstract paintings, and down the wooden staircase that looked like it was floating in mid-air. They crossed the vaulted living room and exited through the ten-foot sliding glass doors, down to a back yard bigger than a football field. Milo had already set up the golf bags on the meticulously manicured lawn.

As they chose their clubs, Mr Fisher's attention snapped to the forested edges of the property. "Is that a deer?"

Milo carefully scanned the treeline. "I don't see anything."

"Mm," Fisher grunted. "I could have

sworn..." He shook his head and examined his club.

Milo ran over to the bucket of balls and tossed one on the grass. "Mind if I go first?"

"By all means." Mr Fisher sat on a marble bench nearby.

Milo gripped his heavy club and lifted it behind his shoulder. *How am I supposed to hold this thing again?* Despite having received lessons from a US Open champion, he'd never really gotten a feel for the sport. "Fore!" With a mighty swing he chipped the ball, sending it sharply to the right.

Fisher ducked, just in time.

Milo winced. *I hate golf.* "Sorry."

"Your stance is wrong." Fisher rolled up his gingham sleeves. "You've got to *be* the ball. Watch me."

He teed up, squaring his hips. "You must envision that the ball has already been hit," he said. "It's sailing through the air, straight towards the destination of your choosing." He exhaled slowly. "*You* are in control. The only thing you need to do –" he swung his driver with precision: CHLOCK! – "is allow destiny to unfurl."

The small sphere soared to the furthest corner of the yard, bouncing across the grass and into the forest.

"Nice one, Dad," said Milo.

"Your turn."

Milo took his place and tried to replicate his dad's posture. He also kept in mind something else his father had taught him about golf. *It's more than a relaxing game, it's an opportunity to get people talking, unguarded.* "So, uh, how is the dig going?"

Fisher sighed. "My workers have informed Mr Murl that the newest tunnel is unstable," he glowered, his glacier-blue eyes glinting in the sunlight. "It's an unfortunate setback, but we shall persevere. We're very close to finding the source of the Nucralose now. I can feel it."

Milo shook the tension out of his legs. *I am*

the ball. I am. The ball. He took another swing and this time the ball flew forward, though it only made it halfway across the yard. *At least I didn't nearly decapitate anyone this time.* "But you said Nu Co. already has more than enough Nucralose for all your products and experiments, right?"

"We do," said Fisher, taking Milo's place.

Milo sat, resting his cheek on the handle of his golf club. "Then why do you need to find the source?"

"Because I have a hunch that all that goo is coming from something –" Fisher smashed his ball into the stratosphere – "unexpected. Maybe even something *unnatural*. And I want to find out what it is."

He sounds like Lucy. It wasn't the first time Milo had thought as much. *Why can't these two just leave well enough alone?* "What do you think is making all that sticky stuff?"

Fisher's lips curled slyly. "I'm afraid my thoughts on the matter are confidential, sport.

Besides, there are some things it's better you don't know."

"Because you think I'll tell Lucy about it?" Milo swung and missed the ball entirely.

"You spend too much time with that girl," his father admonished him for the hundreth time. "There's something off about her."

Milo's cheeks burned as the ball rolled pathetically at his feet. "She did save your life. Remember?"

"Perhaps, but she seems to think that those monsters are harmless," said Fisher. "She could be reporting to the shifters. I still think she could be one of them," he muttered. "And if she's not, she certainly seems to be under their spell."

Milo laughed. "Oh, she'd love to be a shapeshifter, believe me. But if she was one, I'm pretty sure she wouldn't be spending all day and night trying to track them down."

Fisher set up his next shot. "And how is her little UFO search going?"

"I told you, I'll let you know if we find anything."

"See that you do."

It was a promise Milo intended to keep. He knew that the Pretenders were as dangerous as his father said. It was a shame Lucy couldn't see it. Someday, though, he was sure she'd wake up and face facts. *Those creatures are not our friends. After everything Lucy and I have experienced together, she has to recognise that it's true.*

"How's everyone on the mining team doing?" asked Milo, taking a seat on the bench. He needed to get the conversation back on track. Lucy seemed really concerned about her dad's odd behaviour. "They've been working pretty hard lately, haven't they?"

Fisher snorted, bringing his club behind his back. "Not hard enough. Some of them seem to have the impression that time is not a precious commodity. Showing up late, leaving early." Fisher hit his ball high, where it floated far over the treetops before it disappeared. He nodded, satisfied. "And incidentally, Mr Silas Sladan is one of the main culprits."

Is he? Now we're getting somewhere. "Could you take another turn? I'd like to pay closer attention to your form."

Fisher obliged, setting up another ball.

"What did Lucy's dad do?" asked Milo.

His father hit the ball with a tremendous force that sent a clump of grass flying. He stomped the clod back into place with his foot, then set up a tee for Milo. "Sladan," Fisher sneered, "took a day off in the middle of the week. Didn't say a word as to why. Two other workers followed his lead and did the same. They're all on probation now. If he wasn't the only one on the team with demolition training, I'd have fired him already."

"Oh dear." *I wonder if Lucy knows her dad's job is at risk? I'll have to warn her.* Milo wiggled his hips. *I am the ball. I AM THE BALL.* He swung. The ball shot straight up into the air, sending him and his father running in opposite directions until it bounced off the porch steps. "Whoops."

"Maybe golf isn't your game, son."

Understatement of the century. "Dad?" Milo leaned on his club, another question percolating in his head. "Have you ever asked a girl to a school dance?"

"Have I?" Fisher grinned. "I had it down to a science, my boy. I'd buy my favourite gal a long-stemmed rose, pick up a heart-shaped box of chocolates and write her a poem asking her to accompany me on a magical evening. Worked like a charm." He lined up a left-handed chip shot. "Why do you ask?"

"I've been thinking about asking ... someone ... to the Spring Fling."

Fisher sliced the ball, shooting it into the full-height window behind the porch, where it left a web of cracks.

Yikes.

"And would that someone be Lucy?" asked his father.

The armpits of Milo's linen shirt were growing moist. "I don't know," he fibbed. "It might be anyone, really. I just thought it would be fun."

Fisher held his golf club out like a sceptre. "It would be best for you to remember who you are, son," he said. "Don't get attached to anyone in this podunk town. You are special, and that strange girl has no idea what you're worth." He rested the hilt of the club on Milo's shoulder. "You and I don't belong here. Once I've caught up with the shifters I'll do what needs doing and then we'll be on our way. Understand?"

Milo nodded feebly.

"You're a Fisher, son. We don't play by the same rules as the rest of society. Never forget that."

"Yes, sir."

"Having fun, boys?" called Kaitlyn. Milo's perky blonde stepmother waved down at them from the porch, still wearing pink Pilates gear from her latest session.

"Golf isn't my game," Milo mumbled.

"I've whipped up some smoked pâté and crudités for lunch," she sang. "Who's hungry?"

"Darling," Fisher slid his club into the bag, "you read my mind." He marched up the porch stairs.

Brow furrowed, Milo followed.

CHAPTER 6

Mind Control

"How do you define 'trolling' again?"

"Bullying. Baiting. Haterading," Gertie called over her shoulder as she wrote next week's headlines on the whiteboard in a series of frenetic pen squeaks. "You'll know it when you see it, Sladan."

It was after school on a Wednesday and the computer room was humming with energy. Fingers flew across keyboards, notebooks rustled and computer mice clicked relentlessly. The *Sentinel*'s digital platforms had officially launched several days ago, and, as Gertie put it, the people of Sticky Pines were gobbling it up "like funnel cakes at a funfair".

Smitty read aloud from a list of potential articles as Gertie peppered each suggestion with scathing commentary. Tex was out on assignment interviewing the substitute English teacher, while Milo was off taking pictures of the diving team. Meanwhile Lucy, "The Great And Powerful Mod", was stuck indoors at a decades-old desktop computer slogging through the most boring conversations imaginable. *Why did nobody mention that my "very important" job is mostly reading tweenage gossip? Blech.*

Just as Tex and Toli had predicted, SPEAMS Memes was by far the most popular feature of the *Sentinel* site. But after hours of scrolling through threads hoping to slay some bullies, the only troll-related drama Lucy had found was a fourth-grader ranting about a camouflaged weirdo lurking under the Borealis Bridge as if they were waiting to ambush the Billy Goats Gruff. *It's probably just a lost hunter, but—* Lucy remembered the shadowy figure Milo thought he saw out in the woods the other day – *with the Pretenders, you never know*. She jotted down the details of the account in her notebook and made a point to check out the bridge later.

She clicked over to a new, very active thread. *Ugh. Lars. You gotta be kidding me.* She craned her neck towards the front of the room. "Gertie, I think I've found someone we should ban."

"Have they written anything mean or offensive?" asked Gertie.

"He started a debate about whether hot dogs are sandwiches," Lucy griped. "People are going nuts arguing about it."

A curly-haired kid named Greg peered out from behind his screen. "What's to argue?" He sipped from an oversized mug of coffee. "Obviously a hot dog is a sandwich. It's a hunk of meat enclosed in a bread envelope."

"But it's all about the *kind* of bread and meat," said Smitty, flourishing her pen. "Sandwiches are flat. Hot dogs are round."

"What about peanut butter sandwiches?"

Greg retorted. "There's no meat in there."

"But it's flat, so it counts." Smitty pancaked her palms.

"Does that make pizza a sandwich?" asked Greg.

Smitty flung her pen at him.

"Enough," ordered Gertie. "Let's settle this." She started scribbling on the whiteboard: "SPEAMS Sandwich Showdown". "Greg, I want a school-wide poll on the topic by tomorrow, you dig?"

Greg cracked his knuckles. "On it, boss."

Lucy's eye twitched. *No wonder humans haven't uncovered the existence of extraterrestrial life in the universe; we're too easily distracted by belly-button fluff like this.*

Willow stomped into the computer room, dragging her backpack behind her. She was followed closely by Toli Arkhipov, who looked suspiciously cheerful.

"Have you seen it yet?" Toli asked Lucy. He was doing a poor job of stifling a snigger.

"Seen what?"

Willow flung her bag on to Milo's empty chair. "You don't wanna know."

"Since when has that sentence applied to me?" said Lucy.

Toli tossed his shaggy fringe. "Your dad posted a music video on SPEAMS Memes."

Lucy fluttered her eyelashes in confusion. "I'm sorry – a what now?"

"And *this* sock-sniffer," Willow glared at Toli, "has been spreading the word around school."

"What the plop, Toli?" said Lucy. "My dad taught you how to play 'Jingle Bells, Batman Smells' on the kazoo when you were five."

"And as grateful as I am," Toli pulled out his phone, "you really need to get a load of this." He pressed play on a video entitled "*Profound Sound #8*".

Lucy stood stock still as a wave of atonal guitar chords, wailing vocals and intense drum beats washed over her. "This sounds like … like…"

"Like Black Sabbath, Bjork and a dozen slinkies trapped in a falling elevator." Toli laughed. "And not in a good way." He snatched his phone back and sauntered over to his computer. "I will be posting my review of this monstrosity this evening. Send your father my apologies in advance."

"This is mortifying." Lucy turned to her little sister.

"It's worse than that," said Willow. She retrieved a stick of string cheese from her lunch bag and peeled off a strip with her front teeth. "This means Dad's actually serious about us moving to California."

"We might as well move," said Lucy. "We won't be able to show our faces around here if he keeps this up."

"No joke," said Willow. She shoved the whole stick of cheese in her mouth and chewed loudly. "You ready to bike home yet?"

"I wish." Lucy's head lolled back. "I've got loads more troll hunting to do. This job is sooo boring."

Willow sat up. "You're kidding, right? Luce, being a message-board moderator isn't boring. Everyone knows these things are supercentres of mind control."

Lucy's eyes went wide. "Mind control?"

"Just watch." Willow pulled up a chair, rolled up her tie-dyed sleeves and wiggled her fingers over the keyboard. "Pick three people," she said.

"Anyone?"

Willow nodded.

"Jaimie Johnson and Amy Overwhig." Lucy had named the most popular girls in her grade, guilty of teasing her about her friendship with Milo. *They will rue the day!* "And throw in their pal Ticia Cruz, cos she called me Sloppy Sladan after I dropped a bowl of mac and cheese in the cafeteria."

Willow raised an eyebrow. "That was quick." She clicked through the message board to find posts made by Jaimie and Amy. "Ooh, this is perfect. Amy's asking about dresses for the dance next week." She rubbed her hands together. "What should we get them to wear?"

"Primary colours?" Lucy suggested. "Red, yellow and blue?"

"You want them to look like *Star Trek* characters, don't you?"

"Maybe."

Willow smirked as she typed.

Lucy was intrigued. The thought of controlling people who ordinarily made her feel like a wad of gum stuck to the bottom of their shoe was enticing.

"OK," said Willow. "Jaimie's already said she's going to wear a blue dress. Let me just delete the comment that says she'd look better in purple... Doneskies. Now let's do Amy." She googled a photo of a glamorous singer in a frilly yellow frock, then posted it anonymously under one of Amy's comments with a heart-eyes emoji and the words "THIS IS SO YOU!!!"

"This is surprisingly fun," laughed Lucy.

"Now, what do you know about Ticia?" asked Willow.

"Not much," said Lucy. "Other than she follows Amy and Jaimie around like a balloon on a string."

"She's a follower, eh?" Willow bit her lip. "What we need," she said, "is an Influencer."

"Smitty," Gertie called from across the room. "I need that ranked listicle of the school's coolest teachers and I need it yesterday."

"Yes, sir," Smitty saluted.

Willow lit up like a Christmas tree. "Perfect."

She can't be serious. "Will, are you sure you wanna mess with Gertie of all people?"

"Don't worry." Willow clicked over to Gertie's profile. The bio read: "Gertrude K. Lee. Editor-in-Chief. Eco-Warrior. State of Mind." "She won't notice a thing."

Willow quickly searched for an image of an orange ape before a burning forest. In the foreground she inserted the words: "Orangutans are dying in greater numbers every day. WEAR RED to support Wildfire Awareness." She posted it and tagged Gertie, along with Ticia and several other popular students. "Now we wait."

Yeah, OK. There's no way this will—

There was a muffled "DING" behind them. Willow and Lucy turned to see Gertie pick up her phone, then give it a quick tap.

Gertie looked up and saw the Sladan sisters gawping at her. "What?"

"Nothing," Lucy and Willow chirped in harmony. They turned back to huddle by the computer screen.

"She liked and shared the post," Willow said under her breath. They waited for a tense moment.

"Ticia just liked it," Lucy yipped.

"Our work is done."

"It's that easy?"

"Unfortunately." Willow wrinkled her freckled nose. "People's brains are soft and squishy. If you know what you're doing you can make them think up is down."

"I feel evil," said Lucy.

"You should."

First the sandwich debate distraction, and now this. I had no idea humans were so easily manipulated. A thought occurred to her. "Hey, Will, do you think that's what's happened to Dad? Like, his brain is being influenced by some kind of outside force?"

"You think transdimensional fairies are controlling his mind?" Willow snickered.

"I was thinking more like Mr Fisher," said Lucy, gears whirring in her head. She recalled the yellow gas that the Nu Co. drone had sprayed at the Pretender bat. It had made it fly around in circles, as if its brain had been hijacked to stop it from running away. *Mind-controlling other people is definitely something Fisher would try to do if he could, but why would he want Dad to pursue his dreams of music stardom?* Her theory didn't quite add up yet, but she had a feeling she was on to something.

BANG! Toli stood up so fast his chair fell over.

"You OK, dude?" asked Greg.

"I am better than OK," Toli cackled in disbelief. "I am THRILLED."

"What have you got, Arkhipov?" Gertie demanded.

"Principal Pakuna just confirmed," Toli announced, "that Silas Sladan's new band will be playing at the Spring Fling."

Please tell me he's joking.

Willow curled up in her chair.

"Talk about a clickbait headline," said Gertie, her eyes twinkling. "Looks like I'll be attending this dance after all."

"You weren't gonna go?" said Smitty, a hand on her hip.

"I've been to these things before." Gertie rolled her eyes. "It's usually an awkward mess filled with bad punch and worse DJs."

"Are you going to bring a date?" asked Greg, a hopeful note in his voice.

"Oh, please, Gregory. Why would I limit myself to dancing with one person all night long?

That's the patriarchy talking." Gertie rounded his desk like she was giving a lecture. "The purpose of school dances is to network with as many potential high school power players as possible. The dawn of our teenage years is when we, as citizens of humanity, are first able to mould the futures of our choosing." She flipped her pen in the air and caught it. "It's the twenty-first century, people. Welcome to it."

A round of applause scattered across the room.

That girl's gonna be President someday.

Lucy heard the sound of ripping paper and turned to see Tex and Milo standing in the doorway looking like they'd eaten dodgy meatloaf for lunch. Tex was ripping up a lacy pink greeting card into tiny shreds, which he threw into the nearest bin.

"Who's that flower for?" Lucy asked Milo.

"Huh?" A flabbergasted Milo glanced at the long-stemmed red rose he was holding. "Nothing. No one. I found this."

"But you just—"

Milo broke the stem in half and tossed the flower in the bin.

Tex threw a heart-shaped box of candy in after it, then tied up the garbage bag. "I will just take this to the dumpster to make the janitor's life easier," he declared before leaving.

Milo stood in the doorway for another moment, clocking that everyone's eyes were on him. "I'll go too," he said, jogging down the hallway after Tex.

"What's up with them?" asked Willow.

"You know what?" said Lucy. "That's one mystery I don't feel the need to solve."

CHAPTER 7

Shadow and Stone

With a spray of gravel, Lucy and Milo slid their bikes to a stop in front of a decrepit one-storey bungalow on the north side of Black Hole Lake. The house was situated in dense woodland, with no neighbours in sight. Faded yellow paint peeled from its ramshackle exterior, and dusty spider webs billowed beneath the eaves like restless spirits.

"Well," said Milo. The sun disappeared behind a swiftly drifting fluff of clouds, sending goosebumps across his arms in the sudden cold. "Alastair Chelon's place sure looks cosy."

"Doesn't it?" said Lucy.

Milo couldn't tell whether she was joking.

It was Saturday and, after a late Friday evening spent doing research at the public library, Lucy had finally figured out where Chelon, one of the missing Pretenders, used to live. It was a small breakthrough in an otherwise cold investigation.

"And we're sure he's gone?" asked Milo.

Lucy peeked through a darkened window. "Looks like it."

Looks can be deceiving. Milo anxiously scanned the trees around them, their branches draped with lacy sheaths of moss that swayed in the breeze. He had the distinct feeling they were being watched, though he hadn't seen anyone around. But the Pretenders could morph into all kinds of creatures, big or small. *They could be anywhere. They could be any*thing. "What if he *is* here?"

Lucy slammed her fist into her palm. "Then we ask him a bugload of questions." She tromped up the steps and, with a rusty squeal, opened up a screen door that was full of holes and half off its hinges. KNOCK KNOCK KNOCK. She rapped on the front door. There was no response from inside. "See? Told you no one's home." She tried the handle, but the door was locked.

"Oh, darn." Milo tried to sound disappointed. "Shall we go to Buck's Burger Barn? I'd kill for some Cajun curly fries."

"Hold on a sec." Lucy lifted the trout-shaped doormat, then stood up triumphantly, a spare key in her hand.

This is such a small town, even the supernatural mutants don't take reasonable security precautions.

Lucy opened the front door with a SKREEEEEEEEE. "Hello?" she called. There was no answer. She waved for Milo to follow. Reluctantly, he obliged.

A musty smell permeated the house, caused in part by a dingy raincoat hanging in the entryway over a pair of muddy sneakers. Beyond that was a living room filled with faded furniture, an orange shag carpet, a flat-screen TV and yet more spider webs.

What if he's one of the spiders? Milo was sure the Pretender was hiding somewhere nearby. *What if he's one of the* webs?

Lucy flicked the nearest light switch, but nothing happened. "Guess no one's paid the electric bill."

Milo followed her into the kitchen. "Chelon seems to have left in a hurry," he said, examining the crusty dishes in the sink.

"Looks like it." Lucy sniffed and tossed aside a chunk of mouldy cheddar in the otherwise empty fridge. "The big question is, where did he go?"

They headed down the hall to the bedroom, finding a neatly made bed and a closet containing several denim, corduroy and flannel items. The only thing interesting about Chelon's clothing collection was that he owned any at all. As Milo was well aware, the man could grow a new set of trousers if he wanted. *If you had the ability to create clothes out of thin air, why would you buy so much plaid?*

While Lucy crawled under the bed, Milo checked the drawers. Nothing nefarious was hidden amid the man's socks or tighty whities. Atop the dresser were a few knick-knacks, a couple of acorns and a trio of unused bluegrass concert tickets.

"What are you hoping to find?" he asked.

"A clue," said Lucy. "A notebook, an unsent letter..."

"A key to his spaceship?"

Lucy threw a pillow in Milo's direction. He ducked, then meandered back into the hallway.

THUMP.

Milo's head snapped left. The noise had come from a room at the end of the corridor. "Hello?" he called.

"What's up?" said Lucy, dumping a drawer of Bermuda shorts on the floor.

"I thought I heard something."

"Go check it out."

Great. Milo shuddered. Slowly he edged his

way down the hall to a small, windowless den. Inside the dim room was a ratty armchair, a bookshelf containing old board games, and an empty fish tank. *At least this guy didn't leave behind a bunch of dead guppies.*

"There's nothing here," he called. He was just heading back to join Lucy when he tripped on a wool rug in the middle of the floor and fell, hard. Annoyed, and now missing some skin on his kneecaps, he shoved the rug aside. *I'm really starting to hate this hou— Wait, what's this?* His clumsiness had revealed a seam cut into the wood flooring.

Milo pulled up the rug and discovered that it had been concealing a hatch with a ring-pull handle.

"I found something," he called to Lucy.

She thundered into the room, where Milo showed her the hidden door.

"Hot stinkin' clams, Fish, you're amazing!" She hugged him.

"Thanks for noticing." Milo's chest warmed.

Together, they pulled up the heavy hatch door with a "GRUMPH". In the space below was a dusty stone stairwell, descending into darkness.

A hidden basement. Lovely. This wouldn't seem out of place in a slasher movie.

Lucy bounded into the void without hesitation. As soon as she set foot on the first steps, a set of old light bulbs on the ceiling turned on automatically, bathing the tight space in golden light.

Milo nearly jumped out of his khakis.

"These are just like the lights in the tunnels under the Nu Co. factory," Lucy marvelled.

Sinister underground lairs, Milo was learning, were a common quirk of Pretender architecture. "Why does the electricity work down there but not in the rest of the house?"

"The power must be coming from somewhere else. Come on."

Reluctantly, Milo descended, catching a whiff of what smelled like boiled eggs. The air grew thicker and warmer the deeper they went, clinging to his skin like a wet blanket. Beads of moisture funnelled between the grooves of the pastel stones lining the walls. Still sensing the eerie weight of unseen eyes, he kept checking the trapdoor behind them, half expecting it to slam shut at any moment. A shadow flickered across the hatchway. *Maybe it's just a passing cloud*, thought Milo, trying to calm his nerves.

The narrow stairwell ended at a cement-walled chamber the size of Chelon's living room. To the left, a set of tools hung above a rusty red workbench. On the right, a stack of old paint cans teetered beside a dusty cardboard box labelled "Fishing Supplies". But the main point of interest was a large wooden armoire against the back wall. The antique piece of furniture was decorated with birds and insects nestled among pine branches.

"That looks promising," said Lucy. She headed straight for the cupboard and threw open its doors. "There's nothing in here but boxes of nails," she groused. She pawed around in the cabinet, but couldn't locate any hidden compartments. "Oh, come on, there has to be something in here."

Milo noticed some marks on the floor, which gave him an idea, although he suspected that voicing it would prolong their unpleasant journey. He sighed. "Maybe we should check *behind* the dresser?"

Lucy looked down, seeing the scrape marks on the floor. "Ooh. Genius."

On the count of three, they gripped the heavy piece of furniture and pushed as hard as they could. The armoire slid aside, revealing a rough hole in the wall just big enough for a smallish person to duck through. The eggy stench intensified.

"Now we're talking," said Lucy.

Though we're clearly not speaking the same language.

Stooping low, the kids went through the hole.

"Whoa," Lucy gaped when they exited the other side.

The floor and walls of this new, smaller chamber were made of smooth black stone and covered in etchings of sea life. Engraved kelp strands rose towards a ceiling adorned with wavy, watery lines. In the midst of the seaweed were images of swimming fish, frolicking otters and even a couple of octopuses. The floor of the chamber was decorated with dozens of sea turtles, all facing a bubbling hot spring as wide as a beach ball. One corgi-sized turtle was touching the spring with its mouth open in a broad smile.

"Cute," said Milo.

"The last time I saw Alastair Chelon shift into an animal," said Lucy, "he became a turtle."

Milo sniffed the air. The sulphuric smell was coming from the steaming water. "I wonder how far down that spring goes?" he said, remembering the hiding place of the young shapeshifter he'd encountered many months before. "This would be a good escape hatch for someone who can turn into a jellified blob of goo."

"Maybe that's where he went," said Lucy, peering into the spring. "Where *all* the Pretenders went. Underground."

"They do seem to like tunnels," Milo agreed. "Which means they're not hiding up in that spaceship you're so certain about."

Lucy crossed her arms. "Just take some pictures of this place, will you? Then we can get out of here and find something to eat."

"I thought you'd never ask."

Milo snapped a few photos of the spring and the engravings with his phone before they returned through the hole and pushed the armoire back into place. As Lucy double-checked for more clues, Milo headed for the stairs. That's when he glimpsed a shadowy face ringed by wild hair staring down at them from the den hatch. Milo squeaked. The intruder disappeared in an instant. "There's someone up there!"

Lucy ran over to look. "What did you see?"

"A person, wearing camouflage." Milo felt like he might faint. "Just like the guy I saw the other day."

Lucy gasped, bursting inexplicably into a grin. "The troll."

"Troll?" Milo asked, horrified. *How many monsters are infesting this town?* He chased her up the stairs. "What troll?" Lucy had already disappeared into the main house. "And why are we running *towards* it?"

CHAPTER 8

Tall Troll Recall

When they emerged above ground, Alastair Chelon's den was empty.

"Boomsludge." Lucy smacked her forehead. "The troll's gone." *Just my luck.*

"Why do you sound disappointed that the person stalking us has run away?" Milo asked as he slammed the hatch shut. "And why are you calling them a 'troll'?"

Lucy slung her backpack over one shoulder, briefly inspecting each of the other rooms as she led Milo down the hall. They were all empty. "On the message board, some kid posted about seeing a wild-looking dude hanging out under the Borealis Bridge," she explained.

"Like a troll." Milo rolled his eyes. "I get it."

"Precisely." Lucy hustled him outside and locked Chelon's front door, replacing the key under the front mat. "Let's go check it out," she said, hopping on her bike.

Milo dragged his feet. "I thought we were done investigating for the day?"

"We'll be finished when there's nothing left to investigate," Lucy retorted. She thought she heard him mumble something about the Burger Barn as she took off into the trees.

The rough, pine-needle-strewn terrain dipped steeply as Lucy coasted on to the dirt path that surrounded Black Hole Lake. The Borealis Bridge was a little way up ahead – an arched cement structure that extended across the top third of the murky body of water. Lucy braked, standing on her pedals to get a better view, but she saw no sign of the lurker.

Milo pulled up behind her. "Hey." He drew her attention to a jogger in yellow SPEAMS-issued gym gear huffing and puffing up the trail behind them. "Is that who I think it is?"

"It can't be." Lucy squinted. "Tex?"

"Well, well," Tex panted as he ran up beside them. "If it is not the gruesome twosome."

"You're *running*?" Lucy baulked. "For *fun*?"

Tex pulled a water bottle out of his bumbag and took a swig. "I would not call this fun," he admitted. "But I need to be in tip-top shape by Friday."

Milo nodded. "How does your fancy new suit fit?"

"Like Cinderella's slipper." Tex grinned. "Thank you for helping me choose it."

These two shop together now? "What'd you get a suit for?" asked Lucy.

"The Spring Fling, of course." Tex raised a suave eyebrow. "You should consider upgrading your own wardrobe for the occasion, Lucille."

I thought we were going to make fun of everyone's doofy outfits, not take part in a freaky fashion show. "I'll stick with a T-shirt and jeans, thanks."

"Suit yourself." Tex shot Milo a weary look that set Lucy's teeth on edge. "So what are you slugheads up to?"

"Working on a science project," said Milo and Lucy in unison, using the story they'd rehearsed to cover their secret investigative tracks.

Tex pointed at the pair of them. "Can you call it a cult if there are only two members?"

"Very funny," said Lucy. "We were actually out here researching the collapse of the local bat popu—" She stopped dead, detecting a dishevelled human figure in the distance sliding down the embankment next to the bridge. "TROLL!" she shouted.

Tex recoiled. "Pardon me?"

Kicking up a spray of mud, Lucy took off on her bike after the stranger, racing down the muddy trail towards the shadowy underside of the bridge. Somehow the mysterious camouflaged dude had managed to disappear yet again.

She slid to a stop in the mud. *Crudsicles.*

There was a small encampment set against the stony hillside where one of the cement arches met the earth. Lucy hopped off her bike, letting it fall on the ground. She ran under the bridge and took stock of the shabby items: a sleeping bag, a portable lantern, and a few piles of books and magazines atop a "floor" made of flattened cardboard.

Milo coasted in a moment later and regarded the makeshift camp with a look of disgust. He dismounted, then picked up Lucy's bike and set it on its stand.

Tex jogged up behind him, sniffing the air nervously. "I do not smell the telltale scent of troll-kind."

Milo exhaled audibly. "I forgot you believe in those things."

"I told you, I saw one in Siberia when I was a kid," said Tex. "They smell like old cheese and unfulfilled wishes."

Lucy picked through a stack of dog-eared teen magazines and comics, tossing them aside one by one. *This is a bizarro collection of literature for a troll.* Then something occurred to her. *Could Camo Dude actually be a kid?*

"Ew." Tex's sneaker squished in a gelatinous pool in the mud. He lifted it with a grimace, examining the clear ooze dripping from his shoe. "What is this, slug slime?"

"Slime?" Lucy jumped up and caught Milo's gaze. She knew they were thinking the same thing. *Pretender juice.* When the shapeshifters changed from one form to another, they produced gobs of transparent ooze, which meant—

"Hello," said a youthful voice that echoed off the low arched ceiling.

Startled, the kids turned to see someone standing at the far side of the overhang. The mysterious stranger was a tall, brown-skinned boy about their age, whose ragged clothing blended in with the leafy landscape behind him. His face was streaked with dirt, and his unkempt mane of shaggy, shoulder-length hair was so black it was almost indigo. Lucy felt quite strongly that she knew him from somewhere, though she couldn't quite place him.

Holding his arms out protectively, Tex confronted the intruder. "What do you want?" he demanded. "I have a church bell and I am not afraid to use it."

The peculiar boy peered around Tex. "Hi, Milo." He waved. "Hi, Lucy."

Alarmed, Tex turned back to his friends. "You know this guy?"

Lucy shook her head to say "no" but when she looked into the boy's familiar blue eyes, the truth dawned on her in an instant. *Mother of mice. Thingus!*

"This is—" she stopped herself. *How can I begin to explain? "This is the baby creature that Milo and I found at the heart of Black Hole Lake who's part of a miraculously awesome species of shapeshifters that live among mankind undetected"?*

"I'm Gus," said the young Pretender. He reached out to Tex, who looked over to

Milo for reassurance.

Milo was no help, as he appeared to be battling his fight or flight instinct.

"Don't worry," Lucy assured Tex. "Gus is all right."

Tentatively, Tex shook Gus's hand.

The bedraggled boy smiled warmly. "Nice to meet you. Any friend of Milo and Lucy's is a friend of mine."

Milo paled and Lucy's mouth fell open. The last time they'd seen "Gus" he'd had difficulty taking human form and could barely say anything at all.

Thingus has advanced so quickly. A tear welled up in the corner of Lucy's eye. *Our little Jell-O cup is all grown up.*

"Thin— Uh, Gus, how are you?" she asked.

Milo looked askance at the dirty sleeping bag. "Are you living under this bridge?"

"No," Gus laughed. He gathered up his pile of reading materials and stacked them neatly on the milk crate. "This is just where I learn." He held up a magazine and pointed at the extravagantly styled boy-band members on the cover.

"About very serious matters, I see," said Tex.

"It's so great to see you," Lucy exclaimed. "Where's the rest of your, uh, your family?" She glanced warily at Tex. "Are they nearby?"

Gus furrowed his brow. "That, I cannot say." He gently squeezed Lucy's fingers. "But I very much need to speak with Milo."

Milo looked ill. "Me?"

Him?

"I have an important message for you," Gus said, stepping closer to the boy.

Milo took a step back.

Gus's voice dropped, his tone serious. "You must tell your father to stop what he's doing," he warned. "He is getting too close to something very dangerous. It could spell disaster for everyone."

"What is he on about?" asked Tex.

Lucy knew the answer. "Are you talking about the Nu Co. mine?"

Gus nodded.

"Why should my father stop the dig?" said Milo. "He's trying to find out where all the Nucralose is coming from. What does that have to do with you?"

"Everything in this valley is connected," Gus tried to explain. "Please. Mr Fisher does not know." He seemed to be having trouble finding his words. "The source. It is much more than he understands. He must go no further, or we will have no choice."

"That sounds like a threat," said Milo.

"Of course it's not." Lucy placed a calm hand on her friend's forearm. "Right, Gus?"

"I am merely saying what is true." Gus looked around, his nose twitching. "I must go."

"Stay," Lucy pleaded. "We were just about to go to Buck's Burger Barn, weren't we?"

PLONK! There was a noise behind them, like a falling rock. The kids whipped around, but there was nothing to see. When they turned back, Gus had disappeared, as if into thin air.

"Aw, come on." Lucy kicked the gravel.

"Is that kid some kind of circus magician?" said Tex.

"Something like that," Milo muttered.

So close but still so far, Lucy lamented. *The other Pretenders must be close by, but where?* She headed back to retrieve her bike.

"Where are you off to?" said Milo. "I thought we were going to Buck's."

"You guys go ahead," she said. "I've got some research to do."

"Figures," Milo grumbled.

"I will go to Buck's with you," offered Tex.

"You should probably shower first," Lucy advised as she rolled down the track.

The Pretenders have got to be hiding somewhere underground, Lucy thought as she turned on to her forest-lined street from the ring road. She swung into her driveway. *And that means I'm closer than ever to finding them.*

As Lucy crunched down the path leading

to her house, she noticed an unfamiliar beat-up Jeep parked outside. She heard the clack of drumsticks coming from the garage, and all of a sudden her ears were assaulted by the raucous clangour of what sounded like feral cats caught in a hailstorm.

The Sladan family van was parked in the driveway, and Lucy's mother and sister were unloading shopping bags from the trunk.

"What's that racket?" Lucy shouted, dropping her bike by the front steps.

Willow thrust a big paper bag from the local dress shop into Lucy's hands. "We were just asking the same question," she said.

"Sy!" Miranda yelled loud enough to summon a yeti.

The noise whined to a stop and the garage door slid open. Errol ran out and greeted Lucy by putting his massive paws on her shoulders and licking her glasses. Behind him, the members of Silas's new band were set up for practice.

Cripes, Lucy cringed. *I almost forgot these*

bozos will be playing at the school dance.

"Sorry." Silas slid his guitar strap off his torso, then ran over and kissed his wife on the cheek. "You weren't supposed to hear that. It's not ready yet."

"We're trying out a wicked new sound," said an exuberant young man with peach fuzz on his chin.

Lucy noticed the vein bulging on her mother's forehead again.

"You remember Sam." Silas introduced his bandmate. "Best vocalist in the Big Crater Valley." Sam bowed his head bashfully as Silas pointed at a guy with tattooed arms seated behind the drum set. "And Riley. These guys have been working with me over at Nu Co., but they're in the wrong business. They should be making rock, not breaking it."

Miranda's nostrils flared.

"You should talk." Riley spun his drumsticks. "Mr Sladan's a musical GENIUS. His new songs are amazing. Seriously, you've never heard anything like 'em."

Maybe there's a reason for that?

"Nice to see you again, boys. Um, darling," Miranda said tightly, "shouldn't you be at work?"

"We took the day off to bone up for our big gig." Silas winked at Lucy.

Is there a pile of leaves around I can bury myself in?

"Thanks for letting us practise here, Mrs Sladan," said Sam. "My mom's basement flooded, so we needed a new place to rehearse."

"You know where it never floods cos it never rains," said Riley.

The three men all looked at one another. "CALIFORNIA," they said at the same time, slapping each other on the back.

These dudes sound like plumpin' pod people. Lucy felt a chill run through her. *Maybe they really are all mind controlled.*

"Ooh!" Silas smacked his thigh. "I just got another idea for a song." He grabbed a pad and a pencil from his cluttered workbench and scribbled down some notes. "Sorry, girl-illas," he said to his daughters. "When inspiration strikes, you've gotta bottle that lightning." He pulled the garage door shut. Soon the sound of an out-of-tune electric guitar accosted the Sladan ladies' ears once again.

"At least he seems happy," said Willow.

Miranda stormed up the front steps. "I may need to schedule a doctor's appointment for your father," she said. "Just to make sure he's not mentally degenerating."

"You might wanna schedule one for those other guys too," said Lucy. "I think something is affecting all three of their brains." *Milo said his dad's not the one messing around with his workers. So if something did happen to them underground,* Lucy realised, *maybe it was the Pretenders!*

They bustled in the front door and deposited their haul on the linoleum. Errol sniffed each bag, his tail wagging.

Something MEGA is going on in Sticky Pines,

thought Lucy. *I can feel it*. She opened the paper sack that Willow had handed her and pulled out a sizeable cloth item. "What's this?"

"Your new dress," said Willow. She snatched the garment and ran around the kitchen, trailing it behind her like a flag.

"Don't look at me like that," Miranda snipped at Lucy. "You think I'm going to let you go to the Spring Fling looking like you crawled out of a mosh pit?"

"Gee." Lucy forced a smile. "Thanks, Mom." *I'd better find where the Pretenders are hiding, and fast*. Silas's band cranked up the volume, rattling the dishes in the kitchen. *So I can hide there too*.

CHAPTER 9

Flings Fall Apart

Milo unbuckled his seat belt in his father's refurbished sports car, which was idling at the kerb outside the school gym. With sweaty palms, he smoothed his silk lavender tie under his tailored grey lapel.

"You look great, kid." Mr Fisher squeezed his son's elbow. He seemed a little misty-eyed. "Your mother would be proud to see you looking so grown up."

"I wish she was here too." Milo patted his father's hand. "Thanks, Dad." He got out of the car and made his way over to the queue of fancified students at the gym's entrance.

Milling with the crowd, he passed under a pastel balloon arch into a high-ceilinged space decorated with fairy lights and streamers strung high in a cheerful web. Pine branches dotted the walls and a fog machine sent a cloudy mist across the floor, giving the gym the look of a mystical forest. A small stage was set up beneath a fold-up basketball hoop, with a drum kit and a couple of guitars on stands. Overall, Milo was impressed with the gym's transformation, though it still smelled like sweat socks.

He scanned the crowd, eyeing clusters of classmates and teachers dressed nicer than he'd seen anyone in the Big Crater Valley dressed before, although he still noticed quite a few pairs of hiking boots. Over by the coat check, Milo spotted Gertie Lee in an ankle-length green slip dress, holding court for a group of newsies. *Best steer clear of her.* He'd already turned down Gertie's request that he spend all night taking pictures for the *Sentinel*. He had one goal this evening: to dance with Lucy Sladan, as many times as she'd let him. It was such a simple, pure desire that, for once, Milo truly believed things were going to go his way.

He spotted Tex and Toli huddled behind the punch bowl. Tex was wearing a navy suit with no tie, the top button of his white shirt left open. Ever the trendsetter, Toli donned a magenta sports coat over a floral button-down and jeans. Milo ran his fingers through his neatly trimmed hair and headed over.

"Looking fly, Fish," said Toli.

Tex picked a couple of cheese puffs from the overflowing paper bowl he was holding. "Want one?" he said, munching away.

Milo was too nervous to eat. "Don't those things break your diet?"

"He has already eaten three bowls of that junk," said Toli.

"Gertie looks so beautiful tonight." Tex sulked. "There is no way she will dance with me."

"You'll be fine," Milo assured him, although

from the look of things Tex was at risk of barfing Cheeto dust all over his new suit.

Toli tapped his foot impatiently as the hall filled up and the din of voices intensified. "When is Mr Sladan's band starting? This school is in for a big –" he snorted – "I was going to say 'treat', but 'travesty' is a better word."

"Be nice," Milo scolded. He checked the crowd once again for a shock of purple hair.

"Lucy is right over there," said Tex, gesturing to the front door. "Good luck." He raised his bowl.

Lucy pushed through a dawdling crowd of snazzy sixth-graders and made a beeline for her friends. She wore a fluttery knee-length black dress patterned with silver stars. One side of her violet hair was braided back while the rest was down, styled loose and wavy. Her combat boots had been shined and gussied up with pink laces. Even her glasses were streak-free.

Wow. Milo swallowed.

"Looking lovely, Lucille," Tex exclaimed as

she approached.

She grabbed a handful of cheese puffs from his bowl. "You won't believe what I had to go through to get out of the house," she crunched. "My mom made me video-chat with half my extended family."

"I can understand why," said Milo. "You look amazing."

"Oh." She adjusted her glasses. "Thanks. I like your tie. It kinda matches my hair."

"Does it?" Milo answered casually.

The lights dimmed and a mirrorball on the ceiling cast a flurry of floating lights around the gym. Principal Pakuna took to the stage, wearing a bedazzled cardigan over her customary corduroy trousers. She tapped the microphone and squinted in the spotlights. "Welcome, SPEAMS students, to this year's Spring Fling," she announced. "Before we bring out the band, whom we are *very* lucky to have play for us tonight –"

Toli whooped loudly and Lucy elbowed him

in the ribs.

"I want to remind you fine young ladies and gentlemen that, while you are here to have fun, I expect you to remain on your *best behaviour*." She paused to survey the room. "If we have anything like the hot dog fight at the homecoming game, so help me, our chaperones are armed with detention slips and they're not afraid to use them." She glared at the silent crowd. "And now, without further ado, I present to you," she looked at a notecard, "Silas and the ... Sludgerakers?" She shrugged.

"That's the new band name?" Milo whispered.

"Bogged if I know," said Lucy, tensing up.

The students clapped as Pakuna cleared out and Silas and his bandmates came on stage wearing matching denim shirts and trousers.

"How's everybody doin' tonight?" said Sam into the microphone, eliciting a squeal of feedback from the speakers.

There were audible sniggers from the tweenaged audience. Silas gave his bandmates an enthusiastic thumbs-up as he fingered his guitar.

Lucy shrank behind Milo, burying her face in his back.

Sam nodded at Riley, who clicked his drumsticks together. "A one and a two and a one, two, three!"

The drums struck a beat, Silas hit a resonant chord, and the Sludgerakers started playing a rocking rendition of the teenybopper classic "I Think We're Alone Now".

"Children, behaaaaave, that's what they say when we're together…" Sam wailed, his voice soaring dreamily.

Lucy looked up from behind Milo. "They sound…"

"Normal." Milo bobbed his head.

"No," said Toli, transfixed as the song continued. "This is way better than normal. This is NUANCED." He turned to Lucy. "It is like this song has died and been reborn from the ashes of musical irrelevance." Awestruck, he made his way into the throng.

Milo glanced at Lucy and shifted from one foot to the other. "Nobody's dancing yet," he observed.

"Good." Tex munched on another cheese puff. "I am just here for the free food."

"I bet that if two people start dancing, the rest will follow," Milo suggested, perspiring under his collar.

No sooner had he said it, than the murmurous crowd parted like a curtain. Gertie Lee marched straight through the gap towards Tex, her gold stilettos glinting under the shimmer of the disco lights.

"Arkhipov." She snapped her fingers.

Shocked, Tex jerked out of his slouch. "Yes, sir?"

"Dance with me," she beckoned.

Tex's mouth fell open, revealing an orange tongue. He absently passed his snack bowl to Milo as he followed Gertie to the centre of the dance floor. As the pair began to boogie down, the dam of awkwardness broke and a flood of other kids joined them.

"Did that seriously just happen?" said Lucy.

"Crazy, right?" Milo fidgeted with his cufflink. "Um, so, would you like to—"

"Well, I'll be a frog on a log." Lucy's attention had been snatched by a trio of girls with varying hemlines who were passing by on their way to the toilets. "It worked."

"What worked?" said Milo.

"Jaimie's wearing a blue dress. Amy's wearing yellow and Ticia's in red. It's totally *Star Trek*, just like Willow and I planned."

"You made those girls wear primary colours?" asked Milo. "How?"

"The Internet," said Lucy, looking disturbed. "It turns out mind control is ridiculously easy and accessible to all."

What is she on about? Milo decided he'd rather find out later. He inhaled deeply, trying to envision his success before it happened. *I AM THE BALL.* He straightened his jacket. "Lucy,

I was wondering if you'd—" He felt a tap on his shoulder. *Oh, for the love of ill-gotten gold.* "Yes?" He turned round to find a kid his age, though a few inches taller, dressed to kill in a rich purple suit, charcoal shirt and pale-grey tie. The boy's wavy indigo hair was tousled to perfection, boyband-style.

"Milo," the stranger greeted him warmly.

It took Milo a second to process who this person was. The answer hit him like a wave of clear, gelatinous goo. "Thingus – I mean," he looked around, gobsmacked, "Gus?"

The boy nodded, grinning handsomely.

"No way." Lucy beamed. She bounced around the Pretender in a circle, looking him up and down. "GUS, you look flipping awesome!"

Milo felt a jolt of displeasure. "What are you doing here?"

Gus gawked at the festive scene. "I read about the Spring Fling on your school website. I wanted to see what it was like."

"You get Wi-Fi reception under that bridge?"

asked Lucy.

Gus laughed. "Not there, no."

"Then where?"

"Hey," said Gus, pointing towards the kids gyrating as the Sludgerakers played "Groove is in the Heart". "People are dancing."

"So it would seem." Milo crossed his arms.

"I've seen videos about dancing." Gus dug his heels into the floor and performed a smooth 360, looking quite pleased with himself.

Well then.

The song ended and Silas's band started up a slow jam. Everyone began to pair up.

"Lucy, would you like to dance with me?" Gus asked, his palm open.

Excuse me?

Lucy's eyes widened as if all her dreams had come true at once. "Yes," she said quickly.

Milo felt a blow to his gut.

Gus took her by the hand. "We will be back soon," he said to Milo as he led Lucy away.

Jaimie, Amy and Ticia ogled the flashy

newcomer as the pair disappeared on to the dance floor, guessing wildly about his identity.

Milo stood staring after them, Tex's half-eaten bowl of snacks still in his hands. *What in the bull market just happened?*

He tossed the bowl in a bin and weaved his way through the crowd. Gus and Lucy were slow-dancing, his arm around her waist. Milo's hands balled into fists. *He certainly seems to know what he's doing.* They were talking too. A lot. Milo expected that Lucy was interrogating the shapeshifting creature about the whereabouts of his supernatural compatriots, except... *Why is she smiling like that?*

Toli sidled up to Milo. "Who is *he*?" he asked, appraising Gus from afar.

"He's ... from out of town." Milo scowled.

"He is glorious," Toli marvelled. "Those *eyes*."

Gritting his teeth, Milo watched as Lucy whispered something in Gus's ear, eliciting a laugh. *Unbelievable.* When the song ended, they remained together, still talking but no longer dancing as the Sludgerakers rocked out to a more upbeat number.

"What are they doing?" Milo scoffed. "The song's over."

"Jealousy shows its forked tongue," Toli chided. "Come with me, you big baby." He took Milo by the elbow and led him over to Lucy and Gus, who at first didn't notice their arrival.

"Ahem," said Milo.

"Oh, hey," said Lucy, clearly disappointed their conversation had been interrupted.

Toli bowed and held his hand out to Gus. "Would you care to dance?" he asked.

"Sure," said Gus. He took Toli's hand and the pair began trying out moves that wouldn't have been out of place in a K-pop video.

"Great," said Lucy. "Just when I was getting somewhere."

"I'm sorry." Milo stiffened. "Were you planning to foxtrot with him all night?"

Lucy chuckled. "No, but Gus was just starting to open up about where he's been for the past few months. He can lead us to the Pretenders, Fish. We're so close to the Truth of who they are and where they're hiding I can taste it!"

"Don't you care about anything else?"

"What do you mean?"

A head-banging kid with a fauxhawk and a studded choker careened into Milo's side.

"Hey, watch it," Milo snapped. He faced Lucy. "I was hoping you might forget about your paranormal investigation for *one night.*"

"Why would I do that?"

Milo threw up his arms. "Just forget it." He stormed off.

"Fish!" Lucy caught up with him by the punch bowl. "What's the matter?"

"Nothing," Milo huffed. "If you'll excuse me, I need to go to the restroom." Hurrying away, he ran straight into a girl in a tight red dress who was carrying a large cup of soda.

"Eeuurrarrrggghhhh!" Ticia shrieked as the contents of the upended cup drenched her frock with brown liquid.

"Sorry," said Milo.

Amy and Jaimie screamed as they raced over to assist their friend.

"He ran into me," said Ticia, tears marring her mascara.

"What's wrong with you, Fisher?" said Jaimie.

"I didn't mean to," Milo insisted, looking down to see that his new suit was also stained. *Fantastic.*

Amy and Jaimie led Ticia away, firing death stares at Milo.

"Why can't I just have one evening," said Milo, his eyelids squeezed shut, "where everything goes according to plan, where there are no monsters, no Nu Co. nonsense and no catastrophes of any kind."

Lucy grabbed a napkin and dabbed at his lapel. "I don't think I'd call this a catastrophe."

Milo exhaled morosely.

"Hey, do you want to dance?" Lucy gestured at Toli and Gus, who seemed to be participating in some kind of pop-locking competition. "I don't think those two have any plans of stopping soon."

Milo felt a glimmer of hope as he followed Lucy back into the crowd. He took her by the hand, looked into her eyes, and they started dancing. Then the song ended.

"And now," Silas spoke into the microphone, an odd, faraway look on his face, "it's time for something special. Strap yourselves in for a ride, kids."

"Special?" said Lucy. "What does he mean, 'special'?"

Riley drummed a jarring, sporadic rhythm while Silas struck an atonal chord on his guitar. Clinging to the microphone, Sam began to ululate in a way that reminded Milo of an injured dolphin.

"What the freakaholic fruitcakes is my dad doing?" cried Lucy.

Ruining my life, thought Milo, his jaw clenched.

Every kid in the hall stopped dancing, their faces a mixture of confusion and horror. Gus, however, kept obliviously kicking up his heels. As the horrible song continued, people covered their ears, tripping over their fancy shoes as they ran out of the gym.

Gertie was up on a chair by the punch bowl, taking pictures of the whole sordid affair. Tex stood sheepishly at her feet, avoiding Lucy's gaze.

Paralysed with embarrassment, Lucy watched the debacle with open-mouthed dismay. Finally, Principal Pakuna pulled the plug and the music stopped. She ran onstage and physically manhandled each of the musicians away from their instruments with the help of a couple of angry parental chaperones, who then ushered the Sludgerakers off the stage. The gym's overhead lights flicked on and Gus stopped dancing, bewildered by the disruption.

Pakuna tapped the microphone until the man at the soundboard turned it back on. "Sorry about that, folks," she said, her voice strained. "There was apparently a miscommunication with the band. The dance will resume in a few minutes. With *prerecorded* music."

The gym erupted in raucous conversation.

"Well." Milo cringed. "That was certainly something."

Lucy turned and ran out of the gym, her head in her hands.

OK, now this *is definitely a catastrophe.*

CHAPTER 10

A Miner Disaster

"Look, Carleen, I get it," Silas said to the miner next to him. "We're all agreed that the SPEAMS gig could've gone better." He pressed the elevator button, sending the crowded, rickety carriage down into the abyss.

"Principal Pakuna is the one who killed the vibe," Riley groused.

"My boy was at that dance," said Carleen, tucking her frizzy hair under her helmet. "What were you thinking, playing that experimental mumbo jumbo?"

"That mumbo jumbo is ART," said Silas.

Why was everyone acting like he'd done

something wrong? Miranda was giving him the cold shoulder. Willow was treating him like he'd served worms for breakfast. And as for Lucy, she'd flat-out refused to speak to him since Friday. *What did I do?*

The thing was, for the first time that Silas could remember, his life's purpose seemed crystal clear. He'd come to acknowledge a very simple truth: he was Born to Rock. Anything else he was "supposed" to do was just a distraction. *If only I could make my family understand.*

Sam and Riley felt the same way, and all three men were sure that the Sludgerakers were going to make it big. Silas couldn't seem to stop writing new songs. Sam's voice had more range than ever before, and Riley could pick up a new beat in a matter of minutes. It was like all three of their brains were oozing with more musical knowledge than they knew what to do with.

"I don't see what all the fuss is about," Sam muttered. "This town's musical taste clearly isn't up to our level."

"Hah." Carleen laughed. "What level is that? Sub-septic tank?"

The other workers chuckled as the claustrophobic elevator juddered to a halt. The accordion doors creaked open and the dozen miners exited, many grumbling about needing coffee. Fortunately, Silas and his bandmates found that they were so happy, they didn't need much sleep these days.

His head bobbing to an imagined beat, Silas strapped on his tool belt and grabbed a roll of detonator wiring. Placing it on the floor, he unspooled it into the mine's newest tunnel.

They were excavating another cave system today, and Fisher was insisting that they get it done fast. With Riley's assistance, Silas attached the wires to the explosives they had placed in the drill holes.

Silas whistled, clearing the other workers back to the mouth of the tunnel, out of range of the blast. He rechecked all the charges, humming a song he just couldn't shake.

That was another thing: for the last couple of weeks he'd been hearing the most beautiful music in his head. It was as if his brain was channelling it from outer space. And once he'd thought of it, his bandmates could hear it in their heads too. It was some kind of miracle. They'd tried to share one of these cosmic songs at the Spring Fling, but it seemed they hadn't gotten it quite right. *But if any of those kids had* listened *properly, they would have grokked that this is the catchiest music of the modern age. The Sludgerakers are simply ahead of our time.*

His fingers tapping in time to the melody, Silas keyed up the dynamite detonator. "Fire in the hole!" he shouted. He counted down from ten and hit the button.

KABOOOOOOOOM!

The tunnel rumbled and belched a cloud of dust down the corridor. When the air cleared, the miners emerged from the safe zone and began cleaning up the rubble. Silas rounded up Sam and Riley to see the caves that the blast had exposed. Strutting in lockstep, the three men headed towards the craggy hole in the rock face.

"Sladan, wait," shouted Carleen.

Silas turned round as she and two other miners, a bald man with a moustache and a tall, sturdy woman, jogged up behind the Sludgerakers.

"You're not on exploration today," said Carleen. "Mike, Sue and I are taking over."

"Says who?" said Silas, taken aback.

"You know how it is," she said apologetically. "Last time you led the way, we lost a week's work. Just sayin'."

"That's ridiculous. I'm hardly responsible for the instability of the underground topography."

"It's not just that, and you know it," said Carleen, hands on her hips. "Your head's not down in the mine, Sy, it's up in the clouds. First rule of mining is you don't dig distracted. That's when bad things happen."

Do I really seem distracted? And if so, do I care? It's true, I'd rather be up top, breathing in fresh air... Ooh, those would make killer song lyrics...

Silas cleared his throat. "Well" – he scratched his stubbly chin – "it's no skin off my teeth, I suppose, if you guys want to explore first." He stepped aside and waved Carleen and her team through. "All right, dudes," he said to his bandmates. "Let's get this tunnel spick and span." Before Silas picked up his shovel, he grabbed a pencil and a notebook from his coverall pocket and jotted down the lyrics. *Now to think up a tune.* Whistling, he grabbed a spade and started moving rock fragments into piles.

Sam sidled up with his own shovel, whistling and digging to the beat in Silas's head.

"Hey, guys," said Riley, stalking over with a pickaxe over his shoulder and a fist-sized rock in his hand, "d'ya think this is soapstone or—" As soon as he was within a few feet of Silas he froze, his hand at his temple. "Oh sweet, is that a new ditty in my noggin?"

"Get back to work, lazybones," said a portly miner who was so hot he'd unzipped his coveralls and left them trailing off his round waist.

"All right," Riley pouted. "Keep your shirt on, Jeb."

The three men went back to the clean-up job, the new song still floating through their brains. None of them wondered how it was possible to telepathically share music. Though they all had a strong urge to keep this new skill a secret, it felt natural, as if it had always been this way. Silas couldn't help but ask himself whether the world would be a more harmonious place if everyone's minds were connected like this. And it wasn't just the music in their heads. Riley, Sam and Silas were more in tune with *everything*. Birds, bees, wind, leaves, you name it. The world was singing to them, all the time, and the sound of it was absolutely magnificent.

As Silas slammed his shovel into the ground, he felt something shift beneath his feet. *What the—* "Did anyone else feel that?"

"What are you on about now, Sladan?" asked Jeb. He wiped his forehead with a filthy rag.

A low vibration, like the roar of a thousand

lions, rang through Silas's bones.

Sam and Riley shared an anxious glance.

"You can feel it too?" said Sam.

"I thought I was imagining things," said Riley.

Oh no. Silas hustled over to the newly blasted opening. "Hey," he called to Carleen and the other workers. "Something's not right. I feel a tremor. You'd better get out of there!"

There was no response from the cavern.

Silas's skull buzzed as the roaring intensified. "Carleen?" he yelled into the hole. Again, there was no response.

"It's a cave-in," Riley bellowed. "Everybody out!"

"Oh, for Pete's sake," Jeb griped. But the other miners took heed, dropping their tools and scrambling for the exit.

As all the workers dashed out of the tunnel, Silas ran in the opposite direction, straight into the open blast hole. *I have to save them.*

"Sy," Riley screamed after him. "What are you doing? Don't go in there!"

But Silas was gone, engulfed in dusty darkness.

As he disappeared, the ground shook violently and the remaining miners ran, panicked, towards the elevator.

"Silas!" Sam hollered.

"We have to go," said Riley, forcefully pulling his friend back towards safety.

As everyone clawed their way into the elevator cage, the earth gave a mighty lurch and the stony burrow behind them collapsed with a horrifying GROOOMPH, sealing off the cave entrance with a thousand-ton load of rock, dirt and debris.

Sam, Riley and the other escapees coughed and sputtered as the dust enveloped them. Had the cavern completely collapsed? There was no way of knowing. All they knew now was that Silas and the other three miners were trapped deep underground, alone and afraid – if they had survived at all.

CHAPTER 11

Last
Words

"Please, tell me he's OK." Lucy's mother leaned heavily on the kitchen counter, the phone receiver glued to her ear. It had been more than two hours since they'd heard any news about Silas, and Miranda was trying desperately to extract new information from Sheriff Pryce. What they did know was that the cave-in had happened so far underground that it could take days or weeks to reach the four missing miners, whose condition was still unknown. The good news was that all of the other workers had escaped the tunnel unharmed.

Lucy paced behind her mother, the ends of

her flannel sleeves balled up in her fists. *Dad's alive. He has to be.* The pain in her chest was unbearable. *I told him I wanted him to leave me alone. That can't be the last thing he ever hears me say.*

"Now, Miranda," Lucy could hear the sheriff speaking through the receiver, "we're doing everything we can to get to the miners. You all just need to sit tight. We'll update you as soon as we learn anything."

"This is bunk!" Lucy shouted.

Her mother gave her a stern look. "Thank you, Sheriff," she replied. "I'll be waiting by the phone." She hung up.

Tex's mother, Anna Arkhipov, handed Miranda a plate of scrambled eggs with a side of toast. "Eat this, dear. You need to keep your strength up. It is going to be a long day." She and her middle son had shown up about an hour ago, bringing food and moral support.

Tex was in the living room doing a jigsaw puzzle with Willow, trying his best to keep her distracted. Errol lay on the floor beside the youngest Sladan, his grey whiskered head in her lap. He'd refused to leave Willow's side since they'd heard the news about Silas.

"Thank you, Anna." Miranda smiled weakly. "But I'm not hungry."

Anna wiped her hands on her floral apron and poured another cup of coffee, which Miranda gratefully accepted. "Lucita?" She offered Lucy the plate.

Lucy snatched it and shovelled a forkful of food in her mouth. "Can't they just, like, dynamite the whole area until they find them?" she asked, egg bits spewing on to the floor.

Miranda shook her head. "They're too close to the lake. The whole tunnel could flood." She took a swig of coffee, her voice shaking. "This dig has been a dangerous operation from the start. Fisher should have put in place some extra safety precautions. If they're still alive down there—" Her voice caught in her throat before she could finish her sentence. She grabbed a tissue and dabbed her eyes.

If? This was the closest her mother had come to admitting that the worst was possible. Lucy felt as if she were falling down a well.

Someone knocked at the door, sending Errol barking in a baritone fit. Lucy shuffled over to answer it.

"Hi," said Milo. His bike was propped up on the porch behind him. "I came as soon as I heard."

Lucy found herself unable to speak as tears spilled on to her cheeks. She hugged her friend, stifling a sob. He held her for a moment, stroking the ends of her hair but saying nothing.

"Thanks for coming," Lucy said when she found her voice again. Sniffling, she led Milo into the living room.

"Feesh," said Tex, waving from his seat on the weathered leather couch behind Willow. He sounded jolly, but he looked tired. "We finished two puzzles already and are about to start a third. What is this one again?"

"The Great Wave," Willow responded, monotone. She dumped the jigsaw pieces out on to the coffee table; they scattered across its surface like raindrops in a mud puddle.

The phone rang.

"Has your dad told you anything about the trapped workers?" asked Lucy.

Milo shook his head. "I haven't spoken to him yet. He's at the site. I'm sure they're doing everything they can."

"Nice job, Willowski." Tex clapped. "You have completed a whole side already. Do they give out trophies for puzzle masters?"

Willow tapped her fingers in annoyance.

"Too much?" Tex winced.

"I'm sad," said Willow, "not six."

"Sorry." Tex slumped back into the depths of the couch cushions. "I am just trying to help."

"You are helping," Willow replied quietly.

Errol licked Tex's ear.

"*Silas is alive?*" Miranda's voice rang out as she spoke into the landline in the kitchen. "How do you know? Have they found him?"

Lucy ran over to the kitchen island, Tex and Milo following close behind.

"What are you saying? If he's not been rescued, how do you know he's injured?" She paused, her face drawn. "I don't understand."

Lucy held her breath, watching her mother's demeanour shift from hopeful to confused to angry. She strained to hear what was being said, but she couldn't make out the muffled words on the other end of the line.

"Don't toy with me, Sam," Miranda snapped. "Either you know or you don't." She stared down at the counter, her cheeks reddening with fury. "How dare you," she said through gritted teeth. "Don't call here again."

She slammed the phone into its caddy.

"That was the guy from Dad's band?" said Lucy. "What did he say?"

"He was talking nonsense," Miranda seethed. "Absolute nonsense." She poured herself some more coffee, pulled a stool over by the sink and sat down. "At first, he explained that your father ran into the cave to save the others."

Anna gave a rosy-cheeked smile. "Silas is a good man."

"So Dad's a hero?" Lucy wiped a tear from under the bridge of her glasses. "What else did Sam say?"

Miranda closed her eyes. "He said your father is injured, but alive."

Lucy's stomach lurched.

Willow barrelled into the kitchen. "Is he going to be OK?"

Her mother pulled her youngest daughter close, stroking her pigtails. "We still don't know, *mija*. Sam said he had a *feeling* your father was hurt and needed help. He said he could" – her mouth curled into a sneer – "*sense* your father's thoughts, whatever that means. But Sam doesn't actually know anything. I'm sorry."

"The nerve of some people," muttered Anna.

"Why would he say that?" asked Tex, aghast. "Is he just trying to make you feel better?"

"Maybe he does know," said Lucy.

Everyone turned to face her.

"What do you mean?" asked Miranda.

"Maybe Sam really can sense Dad's thoughts."

Miranda looked at Lucy like she'd lost her grip on reality. "No one can feel another person's thoughts, sweetheart," she said. "No matter how badly we wish we could. Besides, if anyone could read your father's bananas brainwaves it'd be me."

Lucy chewed her thumbnail as she tried to piece it all together. "But maybe Dad and his bandmates got mind-controlled at the same time. They were all working down in that unstable cave, right? So maybe they found something weird down there, and it—"

"Mind control?" Miranda's voice had dropped an octave.

Willow and Errol instinctively backed away from the kitchen.

"I am not entertaining your inane conspiracy theories right now, Lucita," Miranda said, trying to control her temper.

But Lucy knew she was on to something. "Mom, listen to me for just one minute. I've recently learned that mind control is not only possible, it's ridiculously eas—"

"LUCITA," Miranda shouted, more a threat than a name.

"Feesh!" Tex slapped Milo on the back. "How about you and Lucy go for a walk in the woods to get some fresh air?"

Mouth agape, Milo took Lucy by the elbow and ushered her to the front door as Anna hurried to tidy up the kitchen.

They headed across the driveway, gravel crunching under their feet as they made their way into the forest. Walking in silence, they passed an A-shaped tree that had long ago split and fallen sideways but somehow found a way to keep growing.

"I yelled at him, Fish," said Lucy, her voice quivering. "The last thing I said to my dad was that I wanted him to go away."

"That's not the last time you'll see him," Milo assured her.

"What if it is?"

He had no answer.

The trees thickened, forming a lacy canopy overhead. When the trail forked, Lucy ploughed straight down the middle, leading Milo off-path through the dense foliage.

"There has to be something I can do to help him," she said.

Milo dislodged a bramble from his chinos. "Sometimes you just have to be patient."

"But it could be days until we know anything."

"I had to wait months when my mom got sick," said Milo. "Before we knew she wasn't going to get better." He stared at a swarm of gnats dancing in a sunbeam. "I couldn't do anything to help then either."

Lucy bowed her head. "I'm sorry," she said quietly. She was about to say, "I can't imagine how you must have felt," but that wasn't true any more. She could imagine the pain of losing a parent. She was living it right now.

"You never talk about her," she said.

"No," said Milo. "And nobody ever asks."

Lucy's heart felt weighted down by a brick of cement. "I guess people just don't want to upset you," she said. "Do you want to be asked?"

"Sometimes, yeah. Sometimes no." Milo scratched his nose. "Not right now though. Now we need to focus on your dad. Maybe we really can think of some way to help him. Like when we saved my father. I don't know what I would have done if I'd lost him too."

"I understand." Lucy tore a pine needle off a bough as they passed by. "I wish I could think straight."

"I know what you mean."

They continued through the wood, a single bird's song striking a lonely note. *There are so many fewer birds here than there used to be,* Lucy lamented. *It feels like Sticky Pines is changing, all at once and not for the better. Why did Mr Fisher have to come here?* Ever since he'd arrived, ripping into the Big Crater Valley with an insatiable greed, the whole town seemed to have been slowly falling apart. *First people went missing, then the factory was destroyed, and now the miners are trapped underground.*

She glanced at Milo, who wore a melancholy expression across his soft features. He was now one of her most treasured friends. If his father had never come, she'd never have met him. She'd never have learned the Truth about Sticky Pines, either. *Nothing important is ever simple, is it?* She sighed as they reached a clearing in the trees.

Milo looked around. "Isn't this where we first met?"

"Yup." Lucy trudged ahead, fern fronds swishing against her knees through the holes in her jeans. "Bigwoof was over there." She stood near the centre of the sunny glade and pointed. "This is where I got hit by lightning, or whatever it was."

"And this is where you threw up." Milo pointed to a shrub a few feet away.

Feeling too exhausted to laugh, Lucy dropped down and lay on the ground, heedless of the twigs sticking to her hair.

Milo joined her, sitting cross-legged by her side. He plucked a thin stem from the meadow grass and twisted it between his fingers.

"We've got to find Sam," said Lucy, her brain kicking back into gear. "He wouldn't have called my mom if he didn't know something, I'm sure of it."

"But what if he's just talking crazy?" said Milo.

"You used to think I was crazy."

"Used to?"

Lucy scowled.

Milo lowered his lashes. "So how do we find this Sam guy?"

"First thing we should do is check my dad's— GAH!"

Lucy squealed and Milo ducked as a sleek feathered creature plummeted down from the sky, zooming low over their heads.

Lucy sat up to see a golden falcon land

clumsily in the clearing, somersaulting to a stop on outstretched wings. *What the— Wait – it can't be...* There was a swell of air as the bird jellified, then grew. Its small body bubbled and contorted as it stretched and lengthened, its limbs plumpening as its head inflated like a slimy balloon. In moments, a boy-shaped figure in a charcoal sweater and jeans stood before them, a sheen of transparent slime glistening on his face and neck.

"G-gus?" Milo stuttered.

"What are you doing here?" said Lucy.

The fledgling Pretender scanned the treetops, as if worried he was being spied upon from above. He dropped to his knees and took Lucy by the hand. "We don't have much time," he said, "but I know how to reach your father." He glanced skyward. "You must come with me now, before it's too late."

CHAPTER 12

The Wall That Wasn't There

"Come with you?" Milo asked the creature. "Where?" *Are we just supposed to trust him? How did Gus even find us?*

"There is no time to explain." Gus rose smoothly from his kneeling position without using his hands to assist him. The oddness of the movement made Milo's skin itch. "We must go quickly. Silas Sladan is injured. He needs urgent help."

"It's just like Sam said," said Lucy. "I knew it." She hopped up from her seat in the grassy glade, ready to go.

She's willing to follow him, just like that? Maybe

she really is under the Pretenders' spell.

"Whoa, whoa," said Milo. "If the shapeshifters know where Silas is, why can't you use your powers to save him?"

"My people cannot help." Gus shook his head sadly.

"You mean they *won't* help," said Milo.

"The risk of exposure is too great," Gus insisted. "There is much more at stake here than you realise. It can only be us, and you must promise to keep our journey a secret."

"Of course," Lucy swore. "We won't tell a soul. Right, Fish?"

Milo said nothing.

Lucy whacked him in the back.

"Fine," he relented. *I have a bad feeling about this.* "Just tell us what to do."

Gus nodded. "Get your bikes and meet me under the Borealis Bridge. I'll tell you more when we get there." He checked the glade for any onlookers, then leapt into the air. With a shiver of flesh and a gush of clear slime, he morphed back into a falcon and soared out of the clearing, disappearing into the cloudless sky.

"C'mon," Lucy called over her shoulder as she slipped on a gloopy puddle Gus had left behind, righted herself and ran back towards the woodland trail.

Milo hesitated.

"Fish!" Lucy yelled.

Laying his fears aside for her, as he'd done so many times before, he ran into the woods.

They pedalled across the landscape at top speed, Milo barely making pace as they bumped down the rocky path encircling Black Hole Lake, not stopping until they reached the arched expanse of the Borealis Bridge.

Gus was waiting for them by his makeshift encampment, wringing his hands.

Out of breath, Milo slid to a stop beside Lucy.

"It's through here." Gus led them across the piles of magazines and mushy cardboard he'd been camping on, straight towards the rocky wall where the bridge met the earth.

Uh, is this some kind of trick? Milo didn't have to wait long to find out.

With a quick glance behind, Gus walked straight into – and through – the seemingly solid wall, leaving a faint wiggle on the stony surface.

What the jellyfish?

Lucy gawped, speechless for once.

"I've softened the barrier enough for us to pass through." Gus's muffled voice emanated from behind the false wall. "But it won't last long. Come quickly."

Lucy pressed her fingers into the rock. "It's not a hologram," she said, wide-eyed. "It feels squishy, like tapioca pudding." She pulled away, shaking her hand as if expecting it to be covered in goo, but her skin was completely dry. "Maybe it's some kind of force field?"

Not even the stones in Sticky Pines are what they seem, thought Milo.

Lucy took a deep breath and walked through the wall that wasn't really there.

"Come on, Milo," called Gus.

I guess it's like cliff-diving in Cabo. Best to just ... jump. Milo closed his eyes, crossed his fingers and stepped through. His breath congealed in his chest. He felt like he was submerged in cold pea soup. But it was more than that. There was an energy fluttering around him, a current that tickled his toes. He emerged on the other side feeling like he'd just passed through a den of ghosts.

They were now standing in a cold tunnel with all the telltale signs of Pretender construction: multicoloured cobblestone walls, dangling lights, and a smooth ceiling adorned with a cluster of strange symbols laid out like a poem. Gus and Lucy were pointing up at the glyphs.

"Those two symbols that look like a Christmas tree and a dizzy lollipop mean 'the Pretenders', right?" said Lucy.

"Very good," said Gus. "You know our language. I'm impressed."

"I can read most of the words up there," she

responded. "I've been studying up on you guys."

She has indeed. And forcing me to do the same.

A faint buzzing sound Milo hadn't realised he'd been hearing suddenly ceased. *What the—* He turned and thrust his hand into the rock behind him. *Ow!* The wall was solid once again. *No going home now.*

Glaring at Gus, Milo shook the pain out of his scraped knuckles. "What is this place?"

"It's a back door," said Gus.

"A back door to what?" asked Milo.

"To," Gus looked around nervously, "someplace underground."

"Someplace?" *He's not very forthcoming, is he?* "Someplace where?"

"What's important," said Gus, "is that this tunnel will take us to the trapped miners. I have never been through here before," he added. "We have other ways of moving below the surface. We only use tunnels like this to bring in visitors. Like you." He gestured at the two young humans. "We haven't done that in a long time though."

Milo had the feeling that the creature was hiding something. *Or maybe a few things.* "So what do the symbols mean?" he asked, indicating the engravings on the ceiling. "I can read them, but the message doesn't make any sense."

"You're right," said Gus. "It is a riddle of sorts." He cleared his throat, then translated the glyphs aloud:

Here lies the way to Control.
Proceed first with feet of stone.
Next, over nothing, with hollow bones.
The last requires many arms to enter.
What lies within must remain concealed.
Beware the Pretenders who enter here.

Milo's heart dropped. *I don't like the sound of any of that.*

"The way to control what?" asked Lucy.

"It sounds like a warning," said Milo.

"I believe it is instructions," said Gus.

"For what?" asked Milo.

The creature shrugged. "Your guess is as good as mine."

"What else is down here?" asked Milo. "Are there booby traps or something?"

"I ... I really don't know." Gus shuffled his feet.

"We can't waste any more time," said Lucy. "My dad's injured and he needs our help. We can figure out what we need to do on the way to rescue him." She jogged ahead.

Gus clapped Milo on the back and gazed after Lucy. "She is an admirable girl, is she not?" He took off after her, running gazelle-like down the oversized burrow. In the low light he looked even taller and more heroic than he had at the Spring Fling.

The boy formerly known as Thingus certainly knows how to craft his appearance. Milo hurried to catch them up.

The tunnel ended at a slab of onyx quite unlike the rough walls at either side. Its glossy facade was decorated with carvings of mythical beings: a unicorn, a pair of singing mermaids, a centaur, and a large, winged snake that coiled around all four corners. At eye level there were two dull, football-sized depressions in the slab, which looked as if they'd been worn there over many years.

What could've made those?

"This" – Gus rapped the stone – "is a door. I'm sure of it. But I don't know how to open it."

"Lemme try." Lucy slapped her hands into the indentations and pushed with all her might. Nothing happened. "Help me," she grunted.

Gus and Milo jumped to either side of her and began to push, but the slab wouldn't budge.

"This is bunk," Lucy whined in frustration. "We need to get to my dad."

Something occurred to Milo. "That message back there. It wasn't written in English, it was written in those weird symbols."

"Weird?" Gus baulked.

"So?" said Lucy.

"They're instructions for *shapeshifters*," said Milo. "We're still thinking like humans."

Gus perked up. "That is a good point. Your kind is not supposed to come down here without one of us."

"So Gus is the only one who can open this door," said Lucy. "How did the message on the ceiling begin again?"

"Here lies the way to Control," recited Gus, without missing a beat. "Proceed first with feet of stone."

"You have it memorised?" said Lucy.

Gus smiled, his blue eyes all sparkles and innocence. "I learn quickly."

"Feet of stone," Milo said loudly. "That's the first clue, so it's probably about the first door, right?"

"Can you turn your feet into rocks?" Lucy asked Gus.

He shook his head. "Rocks are not biological."

So there are limits to their powers, Milo noted. *The Pretenders can't turn into non-living objects.*

This reassured him a great deal, especially as he'd found himself looking askance at everything from lamp posts to lunchboxes in recent weeks.

"Hooves," Lucy blurted. "Feet of stone equals hard feet equals hooves!"

"Like a horse?" said Milo.

Gus grinned. "A horse can be done." He waved them away. "Stand back."

Milo and Lucy retreated as the shapeshifter's outline blurred. His whole body vibrated, then liquefied. The "clothes" he was wearing melted into his flesh. Milo's hair ruffled in a gust of wind as the shifter sucked in air and rapidly grew larger, his slimy skin stretching and squirming in all directions. Gus's torso elongated and widened until he bent at the hips, his hands dropping heavily to the floor. Soon his arms morphed into long, muscular legs. With an effortful push, Gus expanded his neck, followed by his face. Finally, lustrous hair flashed across his hide. He was now a sleek silver horse, with a long white mane for good measure.

Milo had to admit that the Pretender's transformation was incredible to behold.

Tossing his tail, Gus backed up to the solid door. With a snort, he kicked his powerful hind legs and his hooves met the depressions in the slab with a CLONK! The door fell forward and slammed to the ground in a puff of dust. Behind it lay a shadowy descending staircase made of the same smooth black stone.

Lucy goggled at Gus. "That was awesome."

Looking pleased with himself, the Pretender shook his massive body like a wet dog, wringing himself out and spraying clear slime in all directions as he transmogrified back into a boy. When he finished, he looked up to see that Lucy and Milo were dripping with gelatinous goop.

"Whoops." He grimaced. "Sorry."

A slick of slime the consistency of egg whites slid from Milo's once-clean hair down the bridge of his nose like a worm.

Nnggg.

"Don't worry, Gus." Lucy shook the mess to the floor. "This stuff'll evaporate in no time." She hurried to the landing.

As the trio started down the stairs, clusters of tiny white lights set into the walls and ceiling illuminated as if the tunnel was studded with stardust.

"Cool," Lucy marvelled.

They ventured forth, triggering more lights as they passed, their footsteps echoing through the long, low-ceilinged staircase. Milo couldn't see how far down it went.

As they travelled deeper underground, the temperature continued to drop. Lucy, still wet with slime, shivered.

"You're cold," said Gus. "Here." He removed his V-neck sweater – a sweater that Milo had just seen him *grow* over his flesh – and handed it to Lucy. His exposed chest and arms were actually a bit scrawny, Milo observed with relief.

Lucy accepted Gus's freaky woollen garment with a look of amazement. "How did you take this off?" she asked. "I thought it was a part of you?"

"It's like hair, or fingernails," he said. "Like a snake's skin, it can be shed."

Milo gagged.

"Incredible." Lucy turned the jumper this way and that as if it were woven of pure gold. She slipped it carefully over her flannel shirt.

Gus inhaled sharply and grew a new jumper, sprouting fuzzy black patches along his skin that quickly knitted themselves together. When the top was finished, he pulled at the hem, threatening to remove this one as well. "Are *you* cold?" he asked Milo.

Milo was, indeed, quite chilly. "Nope." He stuck his hands in his pockets. "I'm good."

The trio continued on for several minutes without reaching the bottom.

"There must be a faster way to get to the end of this thing," Milo complained.

"There is for me," said Gus. "I'll see how much further we have to go." Just like that, he morphed into a falcon and zoomed down like a feathery paper aeroplane, disappearing into the darkness before them.

Milo frowned. Something was still bothering him about the way Gus had refused to answer questions about where they were going. *Could this be some kind of trap?* "Lucy, I know you like Gus. I like him too. Or I mean, I did, before… But are we sure we can trust him?"

Lucy scoffed. "What do you mean? It's Thingus, for cripes sake. He worships you."

"Not like he worships you."

"What's that supposed to mean?"

"Nothing."

"Hey, guys," Gus called from down below. "You are nearly there!"

Lucy and Milo ran to the bottom of the stairs, stepping into another starlit hallway. Gus, who'd returned to his humanoid form, was staring forlornly over the edge of a precipice. The floor ended abruptly before him, opening into a fathomless gap that extended about six metres. After the chasm, the ground reappeared and the hallway continued.

A breeze wafted up from the void, ruffling Gus's hair. "Next along, over nothing, with hollow bones," he said, glumly reciting the next set of clues.

"Hollow bones," Lucy repeated. "Like a bird. That's easy; we just have to fly across."

"Gus can fly over the pit of despair," said Milo, "but how are *we* supposed to get over it?"

Like the stairwell behind them, the hall's ceiling, floor and walls were made of slick starlit onyx. There were no crevices or crags to hold on to from above, no ledges to traverse.

Lucy cleaned her glasses on her jeans. "He could turn into a giant bird and we could ride across on his back?"

Gus shook his head. "My wingspan would need to be very large to support your weight, and the corridor is not wide enough." He looked to Milo. "I don't know what to do."

Milo was at a loss as well. "Could you turn

into something else?"

"Like something sticky," Lucy exclaimed, examining the walls.

"Sticky?" said Milo.

"Sure. There are tons of plants and animals that can stick to smooth surfaces," Lucy explained. "Like lizards, or spiders, or climbing vines."

Spiders?

Gus perked up. "That is a brilliant idea."

Crackers and cheese. He's going to turn into a giant spider, isn't he?

The Pretender inhaled. But instead of growing four extra, horrifying legs, Gus held one of his arms aloft. The limb stretched, lengthening over the crevasse, reaching towards the ceiling. Once there, he pressed his open palm against the shiny surface. With a series of slurps and glurps, his arm thickened into a plant-like structure, the sleeve of his jumper melting into his muscles and tendons, which pulsated and bulged before taking on a thick, flexible, woody texture. His outstretched fingers became green vines that slithered along the stone in sticky tendrils, wedging themselves into the corners of the walls at either side.

"Genius," said Lucy.

Gus gave his weedy arm a sharp tug. "That should hold," he said.

Should?

"I can swing you across, one at a time," Gus continued. "Milo, may I carry you first?"

"Uh. Are you sure you're strong enough to carry me?"

Gus held out his other arm, expanding his bicep considerably. "I promise I would never drop you." He flexed. "At least, not on purpose."

Delightful. Resigned to his fate, Milo walked to the ledge and wrapped his arms around Gus's neck. Gus gripped Milo's waist like an action-movie hero.

"I need to concentrate," said Gus. "Please do not scream."

At this point Milo was just hoping he wouldn't wet his pants.

Without warning, Gus launched them across the expanse, so fast Milo worried his stomach had been left behind. After a terrifying moment of weightlessness, his feet found solid ground on the opposite ledge. Gus released him and, quivering, Milo dropped to his hands and knees.

CLICK. He felt a square of stone sink beneath his palm, as if he'd accidentally triggered a hidden button. *Oh no.* The floor rumbled. *Is this a booby trap?*

Milo scrambled to his feet, yipping in surprise as the ledge on which he stood began to lengthen towards the other side as if it were made of soft clay. *That's not like any flooring I've ever seen. What kind of mad technology is this?* With a grinding roar, a stony bridge stretched all the way across the open chasm, cementing itself to the ground before Lucy.

Milo glared at Gus. "So you could have just flown across and pressed this button?"

"How was I to know?" said Gus. "I told you, I've never been through here before." He retracted his vine limb with a wet spaghetti sound.

Lucy ran across the bridge and the trio raced down the hall, their footsteps echoing in staccato until they reached a dead end.

Blocking their way was another stone door adorned with a few simple engravings. Each of the door's four corners housed the outline of a different animal print: the splayed talons of a bird of prey, a cloven hoof print, the tail of a fish and a rather large bear paw. Most curious of all, in the centre of the door there was a baseball-sized ring of small holes, all surrounding a pale, round stone the size of a human thumb.

"What's that?" asked Milo, peering closer.

"It looks like another button," said Lucy. She reached out to press it.

"Wait," said Gus. "Don't touch anything!"

But it was too late. A low hiss emanated from the door as a sparkly black substance gusted out of the holes, shrouding them all in a cloud of honey-scented dust.

CHAPTER 13

A Rocky Rescue

Lucy, Milo and Gus wheezed as the murky mist gushed forth from the wall, its inky tendrils invading their mouths and nostrils.

Panicking, Lucy ran back down the hall on wobbly legs, the tunnel seeming to spin around her. It felt as though her chest was being squeezed by a boa constrictor. She crumpled to the floor and put her head between her knees, gulping in air. After a couple of minutes, her lungs cleared and the choking spasms finally ceased.

But it wasn't just her breathing that felt free and easy. Everything – every scent in the air, every sound that vibrated around her and, most importantly, every *desire* in her heart – was suddenly as clear to her as the purest crystal. Everything, that is, except for the memory of where she was, why she was there and what she was supposed to be doing. But apart from these minor details, Lucy was filled with a beautiful sense of certainty. She knew exactly what she wanted, and, for the first time in her life, precisely what she needed to do in order to get it.

It's all so blingin' simple.

She leapt up from the floor, energised. What had she been waiting for? She had *plenty* of proof of the existence of the Unknown, right there in front of her. *All I need to do now is showcase everything I know on a Massive Online Platform, and the world will have no choice but to listen to what I have to say.*

"The time has come," she declared, "for the people of the world to learn the Truth!"

The boys were sprawled out on the ground several yards away, still coughing.

"Gus," Lucy called, "how would you like to be FAMOUS?"

"Fa-famous?" he sputtered.

With some effort, he rose to his feet. For a split second his irises appeared to be glowing green like a pair of fireflies, but as soon as he blinked they returned to their usual icy blue. *Hmm. I must be imagining things.*

"Would you like me to be famous?" he asked.

Lucy nodded. She could see it now. Gus's dashing mutant face, preferably with rainbow antlers on top and polka dots on his skin for added effect, plastered all over magazine covers under the headline: "SURPRISE: SHAPESHIFTERS EXIST – AND THEY'RE JUST LIKE US!" And there, featured in every story written about the Pretenders, would be the duo of adventurers who discovered them. *Milo Fisher and Lucy Sla— Scratch that: Lucy Sladan and Milo Fisher, Cryptozoologists Extraordinaire.*

"Mmm … I don't know." Gus looked troubled. "My people don't seek fame. It hasn't gone well for us in the past."

"But it would be so fun," Lucy implored. "We could all be famous together." She envisioned all the incredible scientists they could meet, the powerful world leaders they would influence, the grovelling apologies she would receive from her many detractors...

Gus scratched his chin. "Being famous could be fun, I suppose."

"That's what I wanna hear." Lucy clapped. Ideas bubbled around her brain in a wonderful fizz of inspiration. "First," she paced along the corridor, "we'll make a viral video and post it on the front page of SPEAMS Memes. Gertie's gonna LOVE it when her platform breaks the biggest headline in Earth's history. Then," she continued, talking faster, "we'll get you on one of those dumb morning talk shows. Everybody and their *abuela* watches those. You could use your powers during a cooking segment and freak everyone out."

"I like it," said Gus. "What do you think, Milo?"

Milo was sitting with his arms wrapped around his knees. "I think we should do whatever makes Lucy happy," he answered with a drowsy grin.

"Awww." Gus clasped his hands together. "And whatever makes you two happy makes me happy!"

Milo's contentment faltered. "It would really make me happy if you were about three inches shorter."

"Done." Gus snapped his fingers and shrank down a bit, leaving a slick of slime on his brow.

Milo brightened up. "Holy smokes," he said. "That was so nice of you."

"Why do you feel surprised?" Gus reached down and helped him to his feet. "I told you. I just want you to be happy."

"Thank you," said Milo. "You know, you're not so bad."

"You thought I was bad?"

"Never mind."

"OK, guys," said Lucy. "We've got lots of

work to do. Let's get started!" As her voice echoed around the hall, she took in their striking subterranean surroundings. Her mind went all fuzzy when she tried to remember where they were. Not that it mattered anyway. *What matters is where we're* going. "We'd better get back home so we can shoot our first video."

Milo sidled up to her. "We can use one of my cameras. I have several we can choose from." He leaned in, lowering his voice. "I can pretty much get us anything we need, you know." He winked. "My dad's sort of a big deal."

Lucy scowled. "It would make me happy if you didn't mention your dad."

"Of course." Milo pretended to lock his lips with an invisible key. "Hey" – he giggled, unlocking them again – "you really don't like him, do you?"

"Your dad?" said Lucy. "He's a total—"

"Dillweed," Lucy, Milo and Gus said in perfect sync.

They all cracked up.

"I mean, I disagree," said Milo. "But it's odd; I can actually *feel* you thinking it."

"It's wonderful, isn't it?" said Gus, pressing his cheek against the cool wall. "Feeling other people's emotions? It's like a cosy blanket made of butterflies."

Yet something was gnawing at the back of Lucy's mind. The conversation about Milo's dad gave her the impression that she was forgetting something. Something important.

"What's the matter?" asked Milo. He and Gus were standing back to back, making sure their heights were exactly equal.

Lucy pursed her lips. "I'm not sure." Her thoughts were slippery, like greasy eels sloshing about in her skull.

"It will be so great not to have to hide who I am any more," Gus chirped as the trio crossed the starry staircase. "Do you think people will be scared of me?"

"No way," said Milo. "You're sweet and kind and adorable, like an otter wearing sunglasses."

"People are going to LOVE you, Gus," said Lucy, casting off her doubts.

Milo jumped in front of the group, walking up the stairs backward. "Is there anything else you need, Lucy? How about a new bike? Or, even better, a car?"

Lucy laughed. "I can't drive." She could sense his overwhelming desire to please her. And there was something else he was feeling that was harder to place. *Hmmm...* She was getting the distinct impression that Milo wanted to hold her hand. *But how would that help us publish a bestselling cookbook of the Pretenders' favourite cake recipes?* It didn't make any sense.

"How about a house?" said Milo. "A big, modern house, with a swimming pool."

"My family already has a house."

"Oh." Milo smiled tightly. "Right."

Lucy's temples prickled as she grasped the tail end of a thought he was trying to hide. "You think my house is too small, don't you?"

Milo flushed. "It's cosy?"

Your face is "cosy".

"Hey, guys, look at me!" Gus turned his hands into feet and started walking upside down.

"Good one, Gus," said Lucy. "That's just the kind of thing the public is hungry for." She turned back to Milo. "Anyway, I wouldn't know what to do with my own house. My mom takes care of our mortgage payments, and my dad always fixes the—" She stopped cold. *My dad.*

The sea of clarity she'd been floating in evaporated as the memories of the day rushed back to her.

Milo and Gus blanched, feeling Lucy's despair cratering in their minds like a collapsing mine shaft.

"MY DAD!" she screamed.

Jolted from their collective reverie, the trio raced back down the stairs towards the door with the trick button.

"What just happened?" Milo smacked the side of his head.

"Mind control," Lucy snarled. Clearly,

the glittering substance had affected their brains, tying them together in a happy shared distraction. *How much time did we waste? Is Dad still alive?* "That dust must be some kind of booby trap designed to ward off intruders."

They all slid to a stop in front of the treacherous door.

"I *knew* there'd be traps down here," said Milo, wriggling as though his trousers were crawling with ants.

"This is exactly what happened to my dad and his bandmates, I'm sure of it," said Lucy. She eyed the white button from a distance. "They must have triggered some of this dust. I bet it kept them from digging further."

"I told you not to touch anything," Gus moaned. "We're very lucky you remembered your father's life is at stake. True terror is the only thing that can break the mental link that bound us."

"That's really messed up," said Milo.

Lucy spun round to face him. "Hold on a

minute. Why do you think this is Gus's fault? He didn't do anything wrong."

Milo grimaced. "You can still feel my emotions?" He plugged his ears. "Get out of my head, why don't you."

"Believe me, Negative Nixon," Lucy snapped, "I wish I could."

"This *is* my fault," said Gus. "I should have protected you better." He held out his arms. "But I can fix this. Take my hand, please." He looked at Milo. "Both of you."

Lucy grabbed Gus's hand. Milo glared at them, fuming, before finally offering his own.

"Now you two hold hands," said Gus.

Grudgingly, the pair complied. Gus whispered something Lucy couldn't understand and his eyes began to emit a faint golden light. Lucy and Milo convulsed as a surge of warmth ran through their palms. The sensation travelled up Lucy's arms, tickled her collarbone, then rose up the back of her neck and into her brain. The warmth spread rapidly around her cranium before it cooled in a minty tingle. When the feeling passed, she could no longer sense Gus's or Milo's thoughts. Her mind felt remarkably calm and quiet. And alone.

"There," said Gus, releasing his friends.

"Thank goodness," Milo muttered.

Lucy turned back to the door. "OK, nobody say anything else unless it's an idea for getting past this thing. What was the final instruction at the entryway?"

"The last requires many arms to enter," Gus recited.

Lucy searched for a handle, knob or lever, but found none. *Maybe multiple people need to push or pull something?* Her attention lingered on the chalky outline of a bear's paw in the bottom-right corner of the slab. In the top corner, she saw the hoof print of an elk, or maybe a moose. Across the slab were two more outlined prints: bird talons and a fish's tail. Each shape looked empty, as though waiting for something to fill it.

Many arms ... means many hands!

"Gus," said Lucy, "can you transform your limbs to match all of these footprints?"

Gus examined the door carefully. With a slimy SLUUURRRIIIIIP, he split his forearms in half from his elbows to his fingertips. Now he had four small hands at the end of four narrow wrists.

Milo winced.

Deepening his concentration, Gus stretched out his hands one by one, until each matched the size and shape of the different prints: the yellow claw of an eagle, the brown hoof of an elk, the silver tail of a trout and the white paw of a polar bear – each an uncanny and perfectly precise imitation of their real-life counterparts.

"Let's hope this doesn't trigger another trap," said Milo.

With a look of trepidation, Gus lengthened his four arms until he resembled a spindly insect, then pressed each of his newly formed extremities into its corresponding shape. Once filled, the pale outlines lit up in neon violet.

There was a noise, as if a mechanical lock had unlatched deep within the stone barrier. With a grating groan, the slab slid open.

A sweet and piney scent emanated from beyond the threshold, along with the tinkling sound of flowing liquid.

Cautiously, the kids stepped through the door. Beyond was a cave that was big enough to fit a pair of school buses. A narrow river of goo trickled along its far wall, disappearing around a darkened bend. Gnarled ropes of tangled wood crept down the rocks and into the stream of Nucralose.

"What are those things?" asked Milo. "Tree roots?"

"That's impossible," said Lucy. "We're way too far underground to see any kind of root systems. Trees don't work that way."

Gus hurried between them, waving a quartet of arms that were still in the midst of reforming to their original shapes.

"A lot of things don't work the way they're

supposed to around here," Milo said under his breath.

On the left side of the cave, glimmering between a pair of pulsing octagonal lights, was a gilded door. A single symbol was etched into its golden surface: a softball-sized circle with five lines inside it, splaying out from a central point like a lotus flower. Lucy read the glyph to mean, simply, "Control".

As she started towards it, Gus ran to block her way.

"Don't go in there," he implored.

"Why not?" asked Lucy.

"Just forget you ever saw this door," said Gus. "You mustn't tell anyone you've seen it."

"What's behind it?" asked Milo.

"Please," said Gus, his gaze lingering on Milo. "Remember, you both promised me you would not reveal what you saw here to anyone else."

"Don't worry," Lucy assured Gus. "Your secrets are safe with us."

Milo remained quiet.

"Come on," Lucy urged her companions. "Let's go get my dad."

After a moment's hesitation, Gus led them to the back of the cave. They followed the river of Nucralose around the bend and made their way into a larger cavern with dozens of stalactites suspended from its high ceiling. Milo whipped out his cell phone and used it as a flashlight, highlighting the hundreds of tree roots that had snaked their way down the craggy walls and into the stream of goo.

Gus raced to the far end of the cave. "They're on the other side of this wall here."

"Is there a way through?" asked Milo.

"Not yet," said Gus. "But there will be." He rolled up his sleeves. "Stand back."

Lucy and Milo did as they were told, huddling behind a large stalagmite.

Gus closed his eyes, a vortex of wind whipping his shaggy hair. When he opened them again, his irises were a bright neon green. Faint lines of electricity sparked in the air around him, dancing across his exposed skin.

Lucy gripped Milo's hand as the ground began to shake.

"How is he doing that?" Milo whispered.

"How does he do any of it?" Lucy breathed.

The electricity coursing through the shapeshifter intensified, so bright that Lucy had to shield her eyes. Gus held his hands aloft, forming a sphere of blinding energy that hovered above his head.

The tremors grew stronger.

Lucy's heart skipped as a stalactite was knocked to the floor behind her. *Is this whole place going to collapse? I hope Gus knows what he's doing.*

With a whip-like motion, the Pretender thrust the energy ball straight through the back of the cave with a KROSSSHHHHHHKKK!

The kids threw themselves to the floor as scraps of searing rock flew past their faces in a flood of hot air. The dust slowly settled. Trembling, Lucy stepped out from behind the stalagmite.

His energy spent, Gus wilted next to the hole he'd created: an opening half as tall as he was and perfectly round. They could see dim light on the other side of the newly formed channel.

"Hello?" a woman called, hoarsely. "Is someone out there?"

The miners. "We're here," Lucy called back, her soul filling with hope.

Scrambling on her hands and knees, she tore through the smoking hole, its sides still hot to the touch. She crawled out over a pile of rubble into a small grotto. There, several shivering figures in filthy safety gear were huddled on the other side, their helmet lights pointed at Lucy.

The nearest one, a woman whose curly hair stuck to her sooty temples, stood and stared at the girl, confused. "A child?" she rasped. "Where did you— How?"

Milo clambered through the opening behind his friend. "Gus just—" he began, but before he could finish, Lucy gripped him by the sleeve and pointed. Behind the woman, a man was lying on the floor. His right arm was cradled against his chest, a bloodstained scrap of cloth wrapped tightly around his forearm. A bald guy and a larger woman with a tangled ponytail were crouched over him, dripping a capful of bottled water between his lips.

"Dad!" Lucy yelled. She raced over, dropped to her knees and threw her arms around her father's sweaty neck.

Silas stirred, his eyelashes slowly fluttering. "Lucita?" he croaked.

"We're going to get you out of here," she promised. She'd never seen her father look so weak before. So small.

"How did you get down here?" he managed to utter. "We were trapped. There was no way out. We were running out of—" He tried to sit up but he cried out in pain as soon as he moved his wounded arm.

"Dad, don't move," said Lucy, fighting back tears. "You'll hurt yourself." She helped him lie back down gently on the ground. "Gus showed us the way to find you."

Silas coughed. "Who's Gus?"

"He's a friend. He's right over there." Lucy turned back to the blast hole, but Gus was nowhere to be seen. "Wait, where did he go?"

"I tried to tell you," said Milo. "Gus is gone. He ran away. We're on our own."

CHAPTER 14

Finders Creepers

"So our rescue party is a couple of kids?" said the curly-haired miner who'd introduced herself as Carleen.

"I'm afraid so," said Milo.

Silas groaned, shaking with pain.

He looks terrible. Milo paled.

"He's lost a lot of blood," said Carleen. "We need to get him topside, now."

"But he can't walk," said the bald man.

"We're all going to have to help carry my dad out of here," said Lucy.

The exhausted workers nodded in agreement.

Milo rushed over to assist them as they

struggled to lift Silas. They formed teams at either end of Gus's blast hole to pull the injured man, as carefully as they could, through and out the other side.

"Where did Gus go?" Lucy whispered to Milo as she hoisted her father's feet up to her waist.

"He didn't say," Milo responded. "I called after him, but he just ran off." *For a moment there I really thought that all he wanted was to help us, but if that's the case, why would he leave? What could possibly be more important than rescuing Mr Sladan?*

Carleen went ahead to navigate, shouting instructions as everyone wound their way across the stalagmite-strewn cavern. When they rounded the corner and entered the smaller cave, Milo's stomach flipped. The golden "Control" door was gone, replaced by a wall of plain grey rock.

So that's where Gus went. To protect the shifters' secrets. Milo was certain that he'd somehow managed to activate Pretender force-field technology to change the look of their surroundings – like the false wall they'd passed through under the Borealis Bridge.

When they entered the long hallway, the pinhole lights had disappeared and the futuristic onyx walls now blended in with the rest of the cracked and crumbling limestone. The miners' wobbly helmet lamps illuminated their journey through the rest of the tunnel.

Lucy led them quickly along. They must have passed over the telescopic bridge at some point, although it was impossible to tell. The long staircase no longer had any steps and was now just a steep, uneven slope. Wheezing and stumbling, the group finally reached the top of the climb, only to be greeted by a low, warning rumble beneath their feet.

"This tunnel is on the brink of collapse," said Carleen.

The crew picked up the pace. Silas deliriously hummed one of his eerie, atonal compositions as they lurched and stumbled towards the bright sunlight at the tunnel's open entrance. Plumes of dirt and bits of rubble rained down on their heads. At a collective run, the group escaped through the outlet beneath the Borealis Bridge and into fresh air, just in time.

With a mighty rumble, a ton of rocks gave way behind them, sealing off the tunnel for good. The miners dropped to their knees, blinking in the blinding daylight and sobbing with relief.

Milo's heart was beating out of his chest, but he couldn't help but wonder if any of what they'd just seen was real. *Did the tunnel really cave in or is this just another of the Pretenders' tricks?*

The next hour was a blur. Lucy tended to Silas while Milo made calls, first to 911, then to his father, then to Lucy's mother. Miranda Sladan pulled up in her van, tyres screeching, ahead of even the ambulance. Kaitlyn's beige Mercedes arrived not long after.

Meanwhile, Mr Fisher and his entourage of SUVs rumbled across the bridge, arriving from the Nu Co. property on the other side of the lake.

Milo and Lucy gave details to the emergency medical team as they loaded Silas on to a stretcher, until Mr Fisher interrupted and ushered his son into Kaitlyn's car. As she drove him away, the boy spotted his father's men surveying the area, taking careful measurements of the blocked entrance with a laser device. Milo lost sight of them as they cordoned off the bridge with yellow tape.

When they pulled into the garage at the Fisher family lodge, Kaitlyn herded Milo straight into the kitchen and plopped him on to a stool at the kitchen island.

"You've been quite the hero today," she said, wrapping a cashmere throw blanket round his shoulders. "I still can't believe you and that funny girl stumbled upon a back entrance to the caves. What are the odds?" She laughed, wrinkling her pert nose.

"Yeah." Milo fiddled with the blanket's fringe.

Lucy's right. Adults will believe anything these days.

"Your father thinks you should include this little adventure in your essays for the Ivy Leagues," Kaitlyn added. She scooped some soy ice cream into a blender and prepared Milo's favourite guilty pleasure: a mint milkshake. Though his stepmother's shakes were tasty enough, Milo preferred the ones at Buck's Burger Barn. There was something about the neon-green hue that just set the whole thing off.

Exhausted, Milo leaned heavily against the pink marble countertop. Though he was physically spent after the events of the day, he felt restless. He wouldn't have been able to sleep if he tried. "Have you heard any news about Mr Sladan?"

"Still nothing, sweet pea." Kaitlyn passed Milo his dessert drink. "I'm sure he'll be OK."

Milo wasn't so sure. He checked his messages again. Since Lucy didn't have a phone, he'd emailed her three times, but it was radio silence at her end. *She must not be home yet.* "Maybe we should go to the hospital to wait with Lucy and her family?"

Kaitlyn shook her head, sipping the child-sized shake she'd poured for herself. "We'd just be in the way," she said. "Your father will be in touch with an update soon. He is so relieved that his workers have been recovered. This could have been another public relations nightmare for Nu Co. The townspeople have only just forgotten about the factory accident." She wound her pearl necklace around her finger. "It's been nothing but catastrophe after disaster since we came here. I swear, moving to this town has been the weirdest experience of my life."

"Cheers to that." Milo raised his glass.

Yawning, he shuffled into the living room and collapsed into one of the white leather armchairs by the double-storey windows overlooking the back of the property. His attention was drawn to the web of cracks on the top-right pane; an uncharacteristic blemish on an otherwise perfect view.

Milo thought back on the events of the day – the long journey underground, the booby traps, the befuddling sensation of the mind-invading dust and, of course, the antics of the showy shapeshifter, Gus. When they had all been affected by that strange powder, Milo had sensed not only Lucy's exuberant delight in her own obsessions, but also Gus's innermost thoughts and feelings.

Notably, despite everything that his father had told him about the Pretenders' hatred of the human race, Milo had not detected any anger or ill will from the young creature. Gus had seemed totally sincere in his desire to make him and Lucy happy. And he'd certainly succeeded in helping them rescue Mr Sladan. But even after all that, Milo couldn't quite bring himself to trust him. And it seemed that Gus didn't really trust Milo either, since he was clearly concealing something behind that golden door down there. *Lucy and I already know about the existence of the Pretenders. What else is there to hide? How many secrets do these guys need to keep?*

And where were the rest of the Pretenders anyway? Milo wasn't sure he wanted to know. He just wished they'd disappear for good, for everyone's sake. *When your entire existence is based on lying to everyone around you, you're probably doing something wrong.* He took a sip of his milkshake. Then another. In no time at all he'd slurped the whole thing down. *How am I still hungry?*

He was just about to head back to the kitchen when his phone vibrated in his pocket.

"Hello?" he answered quickly.

"Hey, kiddo," said his father. "How are you feeling?"

"I'm just happy to be home. Have you heard anything about Mr Sladan?"

Mr Fisher grunted his assent. "He'll survive." Milo felt a surge of relief. "This whole mess is his doing," Fisher continued. "The man's been behaving like a lazy bum for weeks. Late for work. Unfocused. I won't be held responsible if he made a mistake with the dynamite that led to that cave-in, I'll tell you that."

Milo frowned. "Well, I'm glad he's going to be OK." He knew that none of Silas's unprofessional behaviour had been his fault. Not if he'd been hit with one of the Pretenders' mind-control booby traps.

"Listen, son," said Fisher. "I need to ask you about the tunnel you and the Sladan girl found under the bridge. I know you're not telling me the whole story."

Milo's cheeks flushed.

"How did you come across that entrance," Fisher pressed, "and what exactly did you see down there? All I'm hearing from my workers is that they came up through another unstable cave system. But my scientists' instruments are saying otherwise, and I have a hunch there's more to this story than meets the eye. This is the work of the shifters, I can smell it."

Milo felt dizzy. What should he say? *Gus made me promise not to tell anyone else what I've seen down there. But why not? What's behind that golden door? Maybe Gus doesn't want to hurt anybody, but what about the rest of them? What do they want? And what are they hiding?*

Milo pulled at his collar. "I mean, it was pretty dark in that tunnel."

Mr Fisher's voice took on a grim tone. "It's very important that you tell me the truth about what happened today, Milo. Those shapeshifters are monsters. Period. They aren't human, and they aren't your friends. In fact, Nu Co.'s research has revealed some very disturbing things about them..." Fisher trailed off. "Suffice it to say that these creatures are far more dangerous than any species the human race has encountered before. We've learned that they produce an enzyme that is capable of crossing the blood-brain barrier."

"The – the blood-brain what?"

"They can get into our heads, Milo. Manipulate our thoughts."

Dad knows about that?

"Heck," Fisher continued, "they've probably been influencing this town for generations. They could have been controlling the Sladan girl this whole time and she'd never even realise it. It would explain why she's been so quick to defend them, and so meddlesome in Nu Co.'s affairs."

Milo was overcome by a swell of nausea. What if his father was right?

"My gut is telling me that we're very close to finding these creatures," said Fisher. "You've seen what they can do, and you know darn well what's at stake here. Please, son. I need to know. What's really down there? What did you see?"

Milo swallowed. *Lucy says all the best investigators trust their gut instinct. What is my instinct telling me to do?* After several moments of silence, he finally opened his mouth to speak. "Um, Dad? About those caves…"

CHAPTER 15

Shifting Secrets

Lucy lay in her bed, staring up at the cryptozoological posters plastered on the sloped timber ceiling. El Chupacabra. Mothman. The Loch Ness Monster. Sasquatch. *Amateurs. Those creatures are all peanuts compared to the Pretenders.* According to the orange numbers on her alarm clock it was nearly ten o'clock. She couldn't sleep.

Her parents were still at the hospital, where her father was undergoing emergency surgery. On top of a nasty concussion, Silas's left hand had been crushed in the cave-in. Miranda had told Lucy that the doctors were doing everything they could, but she'd sounded worried.

"Babysitting" for the Sladan girls that evening was Tex's eldest brother Grigori, a high-school senior. The door to Lucy's room was ajar, and she could hear the TV downstairs – some old sitcom with an annoying laugh track. If her father had been home he would be playing banjo right now. Everything felt horribly wrong.

Thoughts fluttered through Lucy's mind in a blizzard of anxiety. *How long am I supposed to just lie here and wait?* Her mother had promised to call when Silas was out of surgery, but there had been no word for hours. *How long does surgery take anyway?* Maybe it was already done and they were waiting for him to wake up? Maybe there were complications…

Lucy sipped some water from the glass on her nightstand. *I wonder how Fish is doing?* She hadn't contacted him yet. There was too much to discuss after the journey they'd undertaken. She could still vividly recall the dreamy sensation brought on by the glittery dust they'd encountered. It had been a dangerous distraction, and Lucy shuddered to think how completely her brain had been hijacked by an outside influence.

The Pretenders' abilities were endlessly surprising. She now knew that they could use strange substances to control people's thoughts in order to protect their secrets. Of course, she also knew that humans were in the habit of doing something quite similar. She'd be madder about what had happened if she hadn't just manipulated several of her classmates to wear dresses themed to match her favourite TV series. And as far as booby traps went, the glittery dust had produced a rather pleasant experience. It had been invigorating to know exactly what she wanted and how to achieve it. To feel as if the key to revealing the Truth was just at her fingertips. To appreciate how closely connected she was to her friends. Milo especially.

He'd really impressed her today, stepping up to help rescue her father, even though she knew he didn't fully trust Gus. And when she'd sensed his thoughts, it was almost as if—

BLRRRRRNG. The house phone rang. Lucy snapped up the portable receiver and bounced into a cross-legged position. "Hello?"

"Lucita?" said her mother. "Why aren't you in bed?"

"I am. Can't sleep. How's Dad?"

There was a pause.

Lucy felt the prickle of adrenaline under her skin. "Mom?"

"Your father is out of surgery. He's going to be all right…"

"You don't sound like he's all right."

Another pause. "It's his hand, Lucita. The damage was too great. They couldn't save it. Your father's lost his hand."

Lucy felt numb. "No. He needs that hand. How else can he play music?"

"Or go to work, or cook dinner," said Miranda. "Yes, I know, my love. It's going to be difficult, but there are ways that he can learn to do all of it. We'll just have to be patient and help him to adjust."

Lucy heard her mother sniffle.

"The good news," Miranda continued, "is that he has no other lasting injuries. We're lucky he's alive, and that's thanks to you finding him in time."

Lucy nodded, her chin trembling. "Yeah. OK. I'm glad he's... Yeah." Tears spilled on to her cheeks.

"Take heart, brave girl. You've had a hard, heroic day. Get some sleep. I'll see you in the morning."

Lucy hung up the phone, a feeling of heaviness in her chest. *Dad's the hero, not me. Running in there to save the others when the tunnel was collapsing. But his hand. If only I'd reached him sooner.*

She lay back down, more awake than ever, contemplating a life in which her father could never again play the guitar. The collection of science-fiction figurines on the shelf above her bed seemed to stare at her in the silvery moonlight. Downstairs, the laugh track from the TV echoed through the house.

Huffily, Lucy got up and plopped into her desk chair. She flipped open her laptop and clicked the messaging app.

"Hey. Fish, you up?"

His account remained inactive.

"Fiiiiiiiiiiiish!"

Nothing. *He must be asleep.* Lucy jiggled her heels. Being cooped up inside was making her skin itch. *Maybe I'll go for a walk in the woods.*

She changed into a pair of jeans and Gus's "sweater", threw on her boots and grabbed a few small supplies. As she tiptoed down the stairs, she made sure to step on the outer edges where the wood didn't creak.

Grigori was on the couch in the living room, his hairy feet splayed out on the coffee table. He was cradling a half-filled bowl of popcorn, his head lolled back with a dribble of drool dripping down his blond scruff as he snored.

Careful not to wake him, Lucy sneaked

through the kitchen and headed into the garage. Just as she opened the door, she nearly did a somersault as a large, furry body pushed past her, collar tags jangling. Errol trotted across the garage and slipped under the half-open door, probably scurrying out to relieve himself on an unsuspecting tree. *Rude.*

Lucy ducked out into the still night air. She was weighing which way to turn when she spotted her bike on its side in the driveway.

A tantalising image of the golden door that Gus had prevented her from opening floated through her mind. Where did it lead? Based on the subterranean labyrinth, it was clear that the Pretenders didn't want anyone to find it. Anyone human, that is. But Lucy had already seen it.

I could just take a little peek, couldn't I? If I discover what's behind it, I can use what I learn to help the Pretenders. And I won't break my promise to Gus if I don't show it to anyone else. There were answers there, lurking far underground, she could feel it. Besides, pursuing the Unknown was keeping her mind off her father's plight. It was going to be a long, sleepless night for her, one way or another. *Might as well make it count.*

Deeply satisfied with her logic, she hopped on her bike and pedalled out to the empty roadway, coasting beneath a silent sky twinkling with ancient constellations.

Lucy headed straight for the Borealis Bridge, drawn to the Truth as if directed by fate itself. The area underneath the structure was cordoned off with a web of police tape which read: "DANGER: DO NOT CROSS!" The fresh tyre tracks in the mud indicated that Fisher's men had left only recently. *Those leech brains will be back soon, and they'll be bringing reinforcements.* Lucy brushed the tape aside and faced the collapsed tunnel entrance.

Either these fallen rocks were real, like the ones that had trapped the miners underground, or they were just a trick that Gus had generated using the Pretenders' technology. She'd soon find out which was the case. She reached into her back pocket and pulled out a pink flashlight with a heart-shaped switch she'd borrowed from Willow a few weeks back. Flicking on the beam, she examined the wall of rubble.

She pushed against the rocks. *Blinking badgers*, she fretted. *It sure feels like solid stone.* She pressed her ear against the craggy blockage and held her breath. *There.* She could hear a faint electrical buzz. *It is a force field! I wish I knew how these things worked, and how Gus managed to activate it so quickly.*

Holding the flashlight between her teeth, she explored the rocks with her fingers, probing high and low in a zigzag pattern, searching for weak spots until – *Oho!* – there on the far right, just where the rubble met the real wall of stone, the debris felt … squishy.

The softened area extended along a vertical slice in the wall barely wide enough for Lucy to squeeze through. She was sure she'd never have found it if she weren't looking. She sucked in her belly and, using all her weight, forced her way into the doughy barrier with a SCHLORMMPPH.

The sound of her own pulse echoed around her head, as if her ears were stuffed with cotton wool. Her whole body tingled like she was shimmying through a fizzy marshmallow. After she'd travelled about two metres, the feeling ended and she emerged into pitch blackness on the other side.

She shone her flashlight around the rough limestone tunnel that led to the caves where they'd rescued her father. A loose pebble broke free above her. It hit the floor with a PONK and rolled away noisily. "This tunnel is not on the brink of collapse," she told herself. "It's just part of an illusion designed to keep people away." *But what if I'm wrong?*

Doing her best to ignore the possibility that her surroundings might crumble to bits at any moment, Lucy ran the length of the ruined corridor, then down the rumbling slope that was once a starlit staircase. With no obstacles in her way and no injured party member slowing her down, she was surprised at how quickly she reached the cave covered in tree roots she'd first encountered with Gus and Milo. The burbling river of Nucralose was across the way, still flowing freely from who-knew-where.

Shining her flashlight along the wall on her left, she did her best to locate the spot where she'd seen the golden door. There appeared to be nothing there now but solid limestone, but Lucy was certain the secret entrance was simply hidden behind another force field.

She reached out and touched the stony obstruction, and was pleasantly surprised to find that it was as flimsy as soggy rice paper. *Somebody's already softened it to be able to pass through.* Her heart jumped. *But who? Gus? Or someone else?*

With a hiccup of hesitation, she stepped through the force field, glooping out the other side directly in front of the shiny door, its prismatic lights gleaming brightly on either side. There was no handle or lever to pull, so Lucy placed her hand on the lotus-like glyph at its centre. Automatically, the "Control" symbol lit up in bright violet light. Her arm flinched back as, with a snake-like hiss, the door retracted and slid open with a KKKRRRRKKKSHHH.

"H-hello?" she called out. Her voice echoed as she poked her head into a spacious domed chamber as big as her whole house. This strange new place seemed both primeval and marvellously modern.

The whole room seemed to have been chiselled into a marbled vein of yellow stone thousands of years ago. The curved walls were adorned with a forest of etched pine trees. Below the ceiling, a ring of white light floated in mid-air as if by magic. At the far side of the room was a series of semicircular workstations outfitted with buttons and dials of various shapes and colours. The stone chairs at each desk seemed to have grown out of the floor itself. On the wall above each station hung large, circular screens, all of which were now dark.

That's what the glyph on the door meant. Lucy broke into a wide grin. *This is some kind of control room. Like on a spaceship.*

She ventured into the chamber and cast her eyes up at the ceiling. Creeping along its curved surface like a series of disembodied intestines were dozens of coiling clay pipes. Each one was decorated with elaborate animal engravings. One featured depictions of turtles and tortoises, another was covered in goats and rams. Others were adorned with magpies, deer, banana slugs or owls. *Like the Strickses.* Many of the animals seemed to correspond with the preferred shapes of Pretenders Lucy had encountered.

She recalled the hidden basement below Alastair Chelon's house. The floor had been crawling with artwork of turtles, all surrounding a central grate in the floor. A grate that led underground. *I was right. The Pretenders really do use pipes to travel beneath Sticky Pines, right under our noses.*

The pipes coiled in towards the centre of the ceiling, where they joined into a single tube that opened over a steaming pool of Nucralose in the middle of the floor.

This is straight-out-the-grease cripetastic.

There was a gurgling noise. Lucy jumped back as a large black blob emerged from the pool, twisting, writhing and stretching up out of the water. It slurped on to the stone floor, where it gutterously reshaped itself into a small tanned woman with short hair, dressed in shorts, leather sandals and a floral sweatshirt.

"Mrs Stricks," Lucy exclaimed. It was her English teacher, whose disappearance many months ago had kicked off her investigation and discovery of the Pretenders' existence.

"Lucy Sladan." Mrs Stricks sighed. "I would say I'm surprised to see you, but that couldn't be further from the truth." The shapeshifting teacher shook her head. "In fact, some of us have been taking bets on who'd find us first, you or that rabid CEO, Mr Fisher. Congratulations, Lucita. I owe Mandy Millepoids twenty dollars."

"What is this place?" asked Lucy.

Mrs Stricks pursed her lips. "It's the last place on Earth we are safe. Or at least, it was, until that foolish, soft-hearted boy Gus exposed our whereabouts to save your father."

As she spoke, another surge of goo emerged from the steaming pool and reconstituted itself, writhing and juddering until it formed a lanky man with long braids pulled back in a ponytail. He was wearing a crisp collared shirt and tweed trousers.

"I told you, Twyla," said Mandy Millepoids, when his transformation was complete, "the girl has a fire in her belly."

"Perhaps she should take an antacid," Mrs Stricks retorted. With a slurp, she jellied up a twenty-dollar bill between her fingers and handed it to Millepoids.

"I would prefer the real thing," he snipped.

"I left all my human money in my purse, next

to the butterscotch." Mrs Stricks shrugged.

Millepoids dissolved the bill between his fingers, where it disappeared into his dark-brown flesh.

Lucy gawped at the man she'd always known as the town's popular, if rather eccentric, candy maker. He'd been gone for so many months that Lucy had thought she might never see him again. "You've been hiding down here this whole time?"

"What else were we to do?" said Millepoids. "Fisher has been chasing us down like an orca hunting seals."

"He's captured many of our kin and taken them somewhere on the Nu Co. property," said Mrs Stricks. She strode briskly over to one of the workstations. Lucy followed her, yelping as a chair automatically pulled itself out for the teacher, its rocky base stretching as if it were made of rubber. "We've been monitoring the situation, but we still don't know what he's been doing to them."

She sprouted four more fingers on each hand and started typing on the panel before her with startling rapidity. The screen on the wall above flickered on, displaying a black-and-white map of the Big Crater Valley. Black Hole Lake dominated the centre of the visualisation. Squiggly lines emanated from the body of water in all directions, like rays in a child's drawing of the sun.

Lucy supposed that those lines represented the rivers of Nucralose her father had been mining for. *Huh. It looks like all the goo is flowing from the lake itself. But how could that be?*

Mrs Stricks struck a few keys and the display zoomed in on some grey lines at the top of the map that appeared to represent roadways. A large cluster of bright-red dots moved along the ring road from the right side of the screen, where the Nu Co. property was located.

"Those dots are Nu Co. SUVs." Mrs Stricks frowned. "Fisher's men are coming."

"Mother help us," whispered Millepoids.

"This is not the first time we've been driven underground by the madmen who run this planet, but I have a sinking feeling that it may be the last…"

"How are you seeing all that?" asked Lucy, leaning in to get a better look at the display. "Do you have cameras set up all over the valley or something?"

Millepoids snorted. "Who needs cameras when we have trees?"

"Trees?" Lucy blinked.

"All trees can sense their surroundings, Lucita," said Mrs Stricks. "Sticky pine trees just have the added ability to feed that information back to us. It's really not very complicated."

So the trees have basically been spying on us? Lucy squinched her face. *Yeeps.* Then her ears caught up with her brain and she cottoned on to something important. "Hold up a second. You just said something about 'the madmen who run this planet'."

Millepoids sat at a nearby workstation and

booted up his screen, which showed several dotted lines that resembled the underground tunnels leading to the Control room. "Is it time to rally our forces at last, Twyla?"

"This planet," Lucy repeated.

"I had hoped it wouldn't come to that," said Mrs Stricks, "but it seems we're out of options." She bowed her head. "I hate to think what this means for the future of our cohabitation with the Earthlings."

"Earthlings?" Lucy's jaw dropped. "You just said MONKEY FLIPPIN' *EARTHLINGS*?" She clapped her hands. "Does that mean what I think it means?"

Mrs Stricks waved her away impatiently. "Yes, yes. You were right all along. Technically speaking we're not 'from Earth'." She added finger quotes. "At least, not originally." She clicked her tongue. "The human species has always obsessed over the smallest of details."

Lucy smiled so hard it hurt. "You're aliens!" she cried, her voice cracking. "I KNEW IT." She held out her hand for Mrs Stricks or Millepoids to high-five, but they ignored her.

There was a faint drilling sound coming from outside the golden door.

Millepoids pointed to the dots crowding together on his display. "There are men in the tunnel already."

"I would guess they'll be using explosives at any minute," said Mrs Stricks.

"This close to the lake bed?" Millepoids' hands rose to his cheeks.

"Excuse me." Lucy raised her hand. "I have QUESTIONS." There were so many things she wanted to know that it was hard to choose what to ask first. "What planet do you come from? What's the black goo? Where's your spaceship? How many of you are there? And what do you want from us?" She stopped to catch her breath.

"We want the same things anyone wants," said a gruff female voice behind her. "Trust. Understanding. A friendly game of Yahtzee every once in a while."

Lucy turned to look behind her. The Other Mrs Stricks was standing beside the frothy pool in a green muumuu and a pink woolly shawl. Her wild curly hair was fluffed out like a silver halo around her head.

"Mostly," said the elderly woman, "we want to be allowed to exist in this star-crossed neck of the universe in peace. But evidently that's too much to ask of some people."

"They're getting ready to blast," warned Millepoids.

Another burble of goop rose from the sticky spring, taking the form of Alastair Chelon. "Hello, Lucy," said the pale, moustachioed man. The drilling in the tunnel grew louder. Chelon cowered at the commotion. "This probably isn't the safest place to be at the moment. It might be a good idea to take your investigative reporting somewhere else for a little while?"

"Alastair," Millepoids shouted. "The hour is upon us. We must prepare."

Chelon darted over to another console. The

display above him revealed more red dots, this time on the left side of the map. "They're at the bridge too."

"They've got us surrounded," said Millepoids.

The hovering ring of light above switched from soft white to bright red. Lucy's ears were assaulted by the loud bleat of an alarm. WEEEEP WEEEEP WEEEEP WEEEEP!

"What's happening?" she asked, finally clocking that she was in the midst of an unfolding emergency.

"Fisher is happening," Mrs Stricks muttered, rapidly tapping buttons with her many fingers.

"They'll breach the perimeter at any moment," said Chelon. "We have to slow them down." He raced out of the door as three more gooey shapes slithered from the pool.

The Other Mrs Stricks moved to join him, but Lucy grabbed her by the sleeve. "Wait," she said. "I know a bunch of crazy bunk is about to go down, but I need more answers."

The grouchy woman threw out her arms.

"We're running out of time, girl. All I can tell you is to prepare yourself. Everything you think you know about your world is about to change. Sticky Pines is not what it appears to be."

"What do you mean?" said Lucy. "Please. The more you tell me, the more I can help."

"Help?" scoffed the Other Mrs Stricks. "No offence, human, but you simply don't grasp the situation your species is facing."

"Are you threatening us?" said Lucy.

"*We* are not threatening anyone." The Other Mrs Stricks flushed with anger. "*Humanity* is the threat. Don't you understand?"

"But how can we be a threat to you if we don't even know you're here?" said Lucy. "You've been keeping the Truth a secret from us, and that's only led to confusion and fear. You've built secret tunnels all over the valley, with crazy cave drawings and booby traps. You live right next door to people who have no idea who you really are. It's all a bit creepy, isn't it? Why couldn't you just be honest with us?"

The Other Mrs Stricks bristled. "It was not our desire to conceal our existence," she said. "You are the ones who made it necessary. For countless millennia, our kind lived peacefully among all the species of this planet before your ancestors drove us into hiding."

"She's telling the truth," said the newly materialised weatherman, Carlos Felina, who was sporting a handsome burgundy suit and tie. "*Homo sapiens* are the ultimate manipulators, not us." He hurried out of the door and into the tunnel with Chelon.

"You're saying," said Lucy, the puzzle pieces slowly fitting together, "that we used to know about you?"

"You haven't entirely forgotten us," said a deep male voice. "The evidence of our existence can be found throughout human history." A young man in a ruffled shirt and angled fringe stepped out from behind the Other Mrs Stricks, followed by a red-headed woman in a turquoise velvet dress.

Lucy recognised them. *Kenzo and Marietta Corbin.*

Marietta wiped the slime from her neck with a lace handkerchief she conjured into existence. "Stories of our kind are ingrained in the legends you tell," she said, "the rituals you follow, the dreams you dream."

"Sea monsters," said Kenzo, "unicorns, mermaids, dragons, missing links, talking snakes, chupacabras, goblins, leprechauns, fairies – shapeshifters."

Lucy gaped, a chill coursing down her arms and legs. "Wait a bug-blinking minute... You're saying all those mythical and cryptozoological creatures are real? All of it? *Everything?*"

"It's all real," said the Other Mrs Stricks. "Just not the way people think it is."

Another blob congealed into a man wearing a flannel shirt over a pot belly, a faded baseball cap atop his goateed head.

"Goosie!" Scruffy Steve Kozlowski greeted Lucy. Before his true nature had been exposed, he'd been the drummer in Silas's former band, The Sticky Six, for many years. "Any news on your dad? I heard he was hurt pretty bad."

The ground lurched, throwing everyone to their knees. Steve scrambled up to take his place at a console beside Mrs Stricks.

"Fisher's forces are amassing on the bridge," shouted Chelon. "Man your stations."

"How long have you been on our planet?" Lucy yelled over the din. "Hundreds of years? Thousands?"

"*Millions*," said Marietta Corbin. "Long before your kind ever came into being."

"Without us," snipped the Other Mrs Stricks, "I daresay you *Pretenders* would still be walking on four legs."

The deafening RATATATATATAT of a jackhammer in the tunnel drowned out the rapid thrum of Lucy's heart.

"Walking on… Pretenders…?" *What are these crayliens talking about?* Lucy shook her head. "No. *You're* the Pretenders."

Marietta and the Other Mrs Stricks stared at the girl in bewilderment.

"Aren't you?" Lucy asked, a little meekly.

The Other Mrs Stricks approached, her large frame looming over the girl. "You don't understand at all, do you? *We* are not the Pretenders. *You* are."

Lucy staggered back. "But what about those warning signs you wrote all over the valley? 'Beware the Pretenders.' That's you. Because you *pretend* to be animals and people, but you're not, you're really made up of black globby stuff."

"Why would we warn ourselves about ourselves?" Mrs Stricks shouted from her station. The dots on her screen were marching through the tunnel on her map like angry red ants.

"We have been known by many names on many planets," said the Other Mrs Stricks. "The Ancient Ones. The Eternals. The Protectors of Life. We call ourselves the Nagalons, and we've been around longer than you could possibly imagine."

Lucy's head felt like it was bursting into a bajillion pieces. "But why?" she asked. "Why do you call *us* Pretenders?"

"Because ever since you humans forgot what you were," said the older woman, "since you began pretending to be something you're not, you've been absolutely impossible to live with."

"And what have we been pretending to be?" Lucy demanded.

"The centre of the universe."

The golden door hissed open, letting in a plume of smoke that smelled of sulphur. Coughing, Alastair Chelon and Carlos Felina tore into the room.

"Incoming!" Felina cried.

Mrs Stricks leapt out of her chair and dived for Lucy, shielding her with her body as a massive explosion rang out from the tunnel system, shooting rocks and debris in all directions. The clay pipes crumbled to dust as a fire erupted from Millepoids' console. Lucy could hear the thunderous sound of rushing water as the earth trembled around them, shaking the chamber so violently that she was sure they were all about to shatter, just like all her illusions about the history of mankind.

CHAPTER 16

Glug Glug
Glug

Milo heard the explosion from half a mile away. *Nattering Nasdaq, what was that?* He pulled his bike to the side of the ring road and gazed at the column of smoke rising above the treeline at the north side of Black Hole Lake. A sick feeling trickled up his throat. *What has Dad done?* Panting, he cycled along the wooded edge of the asphalt at top speed, heading for the Borealis Bridge.

Like Lucy, Milo had been unable to sleep, but his insomnia had been caused by a mixture of confusion and guilt. He'd seen her messages when she'd sent them, but he couldn't bring himself to respond. Not after everything he'd told his father.

"Dad," Milo had said after describing the mysterious golden door, "do you think that's where—"

"The monsters have been hiding all this time?" said Mr Fisher. Milo tensed as he heard his father chuckle on the other end of the line. "You've done well, son. My team will have to act fast. Give yourself a pat on the back, kiddo. You're a hero twice over today. By tomorrow, we'll be looking at a whole new world."

"What are you going to do to—" Milo began, but his father had already hung up the phone.

Milo knew Lucy would never understand what he'd done. What he'd had to do. *What? Was I supposed to lie to my own father to protect the shifters? They're not like us. They're dangerous. And what, should I have kept my promise to Gus? He's not really my friend, is he? I mean, I wouldn't say he's evil or anything. But can he be trusted? No.*

Mankind is better safe than sorry. It's us versus them. Humans versus non-humans. Right? These questions and more rattled around in his brain as he lay in his four-poster bed in his meticulously tidy bedroom. *I did the right thing. Didn't I?* He couldn't be sure he knew the answer.

Twenty minutes after Lucy messaged him, Milo had finally worked up the nerve to respond.

"Hey," he said. "I'm here."

But she didn't answer. Milo knew better than to assume she'd simply gone to bed. *She wouldn't have headed back to the tunnel to investigate, would she?* He sat bolt upright. "Yes", was the answer. That's precisely what she'd do.

Frantically, he texted his father. "Uh, Dad? You're not planning on doing anything *drastic* down in the tunnel tonight, are you?" Again, he waited for an answer that never came. Worried that Lucy was about to become caught up in the impending clash between Nu Co.'s security specialists and a clan of unpredictable freaks, Milo threw on a long-sleeved shirt, raced out of the door and was on his bike before the hour struck eleven.

He was nearing the turn-off to the bridge when he encountered a blockade formed by a trio of Nu Co.'s windowless white vans. *I guess I won't be going that way.* He veered off the asphalt and coasted bumpily through the woods, sliding to a stop at the edge of a ridge overlooking the lake. Hands trembling, he pulled out a pair of binoculars from his rucksack. What he saw made his stomach turn.

Moonlit smoke billowed from the tunnel entrance beneath the Borealis Bridge, pouring straight through the force field of "rubble" that was blinking in and out of existence like a half-tuned radio station. Nine drones hovered overhead, shining spotlights on the path below where a force of fifty-odd men in midnight-blue tactical uniforms were arranged like an army of action figures, their weapons raised. *They've come for the creatures.* Milo's breath escaped in a choked whistle. *I really hope*

Lucy's not down there.

A brigade of SUVs were parked above Gus's former encampment. Milo suspected that his father was inside one of them.

Shouldn't somebody be trying to put out whatever's causing all that smoke?

He scanned the rest of the mottled shore from his elevated position on the ridge and noticed something strange about the lake itself. *What in the world is happening down there?* The water level was much lower than he'd ever seen it. There was at least twenty more metres of muddy beachfront now exposed, leaving dank puddles glittering in the low light. *Is the lake draining?*

With a knot of dread in his stomach, Milo kicked off the ridge and steered chaotically down the steep embankment, hitting shrubs and brambles as often as he avoided them. He ditched his bike and backpack behind a bush and, picking burrs out of his trousers, crouched in the shadows a few yards behind the rear guard of his father's waiting battalion. When he was sure no one was looking, he darted across the track and tiptoed into the muck of the rapidly widening shore.

The lake gurgled and churned as the water continued to drain away. Milo slid to a stop on the soggy beach, which now ended at a sheer vertical drop. *Chittering Cheneys.* He looked out at the newly revealed crater. He'd known Black Hole Lake was deep, but he hadn't appreciated that it was literally situated in a big – well – HOLE.

He knelt by the ledge and peered at the murky water far below. It was receding at an alarming pace. He picked up a stone and dropped it in. It took three full Mississippis before he heard a splash. *This whole basin will be empty in a matter of minutes. Just how big was that underground explosion?*

Back at the bridge, a dozen men in ebony suits were lined up along the guardrail, puffs of smoke swirling around them. Mr Fisher stood in the middle of the team, a bullhorn gripped tightly in his hand.

Milo dashed back towards the brightly lit path and hid behind a large boulder that was lodged in the mire not far from the crater's edge. From there he had a good view of the hazy archway.

Mr Fisher switched on his megaphone with a tinny whine. "Attention, shifters," he declared. "Our sensors have detected you at the entrance to your underground lair. We have you completely surrounded. Exit the tunnel now, and make no sudden moves."

Milo watched uneasily as the false wall of rubble flickered out of existence. Mandy Millepoids was the first to emerge. He strode through the curtain of smoke, a rattle of cocking weaponry flowing out from the security force before him.

"What is this, Fisher?" Millepoids shouted up at the bridge. "For months now we've left you and your company alone. All we ask is that you respect our rights and do the same for us. There is no need for this confrontation to escalate. Leave us in peace, we beg you."

Mr Fisher waved him on. "That's it, Mr Millepoids. Keep walking. When everyone has come out of hiding I'll tell you what's going to happen next."

Head held high, Millepoids complied. He marched out on to the byway, towards the line of helmeted men. Their dart guns were readied, loaded with biochemical Nucralose-derived substances – weaponry that Milo had previously seen work to prevent the shapeshifters from changing form, and much worse.

Behind Millepoids, the Strickses emerged from under the bridge, squinting under the criss-crossed drone spotlights. Between them they carried a coughing Lucy by her armpits.

Milo's heart leapt into his throat. *She is here. Is she all right? Run, Lucy! You've got to get out of there.*

"You have the Sladan girl," said Fisher. "Is she being held hostage?"

"Hostage?" scoffed the Other Mrs Stricks.

Lucy twisted out of the Strickses' grip and made a rude gesture at the men on the bridge. "Why don't you go blow out some birthday candles, ya dinked-up donkey," she yelled at Fisher.

Milo dug his fingers in his hair. *What is she doing?*

Fisher glowered down at her. "I suspected as much. Suit yourself. As for everybody else," he barked into his megaphone, "show yourselves."

Chelon, Kozlowski and Felina strode out of the tunnel with their arms raised. The Corbins followed behind, walking hand in hand, their faces drawn.

Lucy indicated the creatures around her as she addressed Fisher. "These people don't want to hurt anybody. They've been here for a gazillion years already. They just want to exist in peace."

"I'll try to remember that the next time they attempt to thrust me into oblivion," Fisher responded. "The time has come for you to choose sides, Miss Sladan. Are you one of us, or one of them?"

"Well, I certainly know what I'm not," Lucy jutted out her chin, "and that's anything like *you*." She turned and rejoined the Strickses, who pulled her into the centre of the throng.

Lucy Sladan, why can't you just make a smart, rational, normal *decision for once?*

GKLRRGGKLRRGGKLRRGGKLRRGG.

A thunderous gurgle erupted from the lake. Skipping out from his sheltered spot, Milo scurried down the beach to the edge of the immense, almost perfectly round crater at the heart of Sticky Pines. He baulked at the depth of the drop before him – easily the length of two football fields. *Moneygrubbing Mercers, this lake is nearly empty.*

Out in middle of the crater, a tall conical pillar of rock held up a small island known as the Siren's Lair – the place where Milo and Lucy had first found Gus. Moonlight glinted off the water far below, churning as it was siphoned away from the exposed lake bottom, revealing mud, boulders, rotting tree stumps and scores of flopping fish.

Abruptly, a giant sucking sound rang out from the depths of the pit, like a thousand straws hoovering up the largest, thickest milkshake the world had ever seen. With a XXXXXLLLLLPPPPPPP! all the debris at the bottom of the lake vanished at once, as if absorbed by a giant sponge. Milo gaped at the abyss, astonished by what he'd just seen – and by what had just been revealed.

What. The actual. Bunk.

There, once concealed by the steaming, murky waters of Black Hole Lake, was a massive, quivering blob of iridescent black goo nearly as big as the mile-wide crater itself. A pearly purple vibration rippled across its blubbery surface and the rocky pedestal that held the Siren's Lair aloft crumbled from the bottom up. The island tilted, then tumbled, its boulders and logs and trees somersaulting in mid-air until they crashed cacophonously into the outsized mass below. The blob shivered as the cascade of island detritus hit its rubbery exterior – then it swallowed each stone, bush and branch in a series of ravenous SLURPS, absorbing every piece of matter until no trace of the island was left.

For a moment, Milo forgot to breathe. *Whelp. This isn't good.*

CHAPTER 17

The Origin

"What on Earth is that?!"

"Good lord!"

"It's the Nucralose mother lode."

Lucy heard the shocked cries of Fisher's flunkies atop the Borealis Bridge. Through the haze of smoke from the underground fire, she spotted the men in sharp suits taking off their sunglasses, utterly mesmerised by what they saw. *What are those toerags gawping at?*

With a grunt, she pushed herself through the cluster of alien Sticky Pineseans, noting the Nu Co. soldiers positioned on either side of the walkway with their dart guns poised and ready to fire. Lucy knew that the engineered bioweapons they carried could horribly disrupt the Nagalons' powers. She also knew that the Nagalons were perfectly capable of defending themselves against an organised attack. But Nu Co.'s forces seemed better equipped than she'd ever seen them before. There were at least three dozen tactical mercenaries, not to mention the security team on the bridge and the drones hovering up above.

Do the aliens actually stand a chance?

Lucy stepped through the cluster of shapeshifters to see what all the fuss was about. With a shock, she grasped that the basin was completely dry. *When Fisher's men blasted the tunnel, they must have broken right through the lake bed.* Then Lucy noticed something bulging out of the depths of the crater that knocked the breath from her chest. *What is that big, black, blubbery BLOB?*

The shapeshifters had noticed the drained lake as well. Kenzo and Marietta whispered urgently to Scruffy Steve, while Carlos Felina paced in an anxious circle. Meanwhile, the Strickses regarded Mr Fisher as if they wanted to grind him into hamburger meat.

"What on the round blue Earth is that humongous ball of goo?" asked Lucy.

The Other Mrs Stricks bowed her head solemnly. "It is something sacred that should never have been disturbed."

"But what *is* it?" Lucy pressed.

"Well" – Mrs Stricks sighed – "you did want to see our spaceship, didn't you?"

Lucy nearly fell over backward. "There's a spaceship inside that giant glob of gunk?"

Wincing, Mrs Stricks shook her head. "No, Lucita. You don't understand. The blob *is* our spaceship."

"No. Flippin'. Way." Lucy jumped up to catch another glimpse of the intergalactic jelly mould.

"Don't confuse the girl, Twyla," the Other Mrs Stricks scolded. "The Origin is not a ship."

"It *is* how we travel, dear," snipped Mrs Stricks.

"But it's so much more than that," said Marietta. "It is our mother and our father. It is the genesis of our creation."

The Origin. Lucy's eyes widened as she took in what they were saying. "You crawled out of that thing?" she said. "Up through the lake?"

Millepoids nodded reverently, his long braids whipping around in the breeze brought on by the buzzing drone propellers. "Every one of us."

"Miniblobs out of the Megablob," Lucy marvelled. "How does it travel through space? Does it blast off like a rocket?"

"I wish it were that easy," said Mrs Stricks, catching a warning look from the Other Mrs Stricks.

Carlos Felina stormed past. "We must enact our exit strategy immediately. It's time to leave the planet."

"Don't say that," Marietta hushed him. "Earth has been our home for aeons. There must be a way to peacefully resolve things with the humans."

"Look around you." Felina gestured at the armed squadron that surrounded them. "These men won't stop until our kind is completely destroyed. If we want to live, we need to leave. Now."

The screech of Fisher's megaphone echoed around the lakefront. "So this is what you've been protecting, is it?" he boomed from his vantage point atop the bridge. "I'll bet that behemoth down there is the source of all the Nucralose in the Big Crater Valley." He spoke as if his wildest dreams were finally manifesting. "The size of it. It's virtually limitless."

"It doesn't belong to you," yelled Millepoids.

Fisher's confidence never faltered. "According to our laws, I have as much right to claim these riches as any other member of the *human race*."

There was a humming commotion overhead as Fisher's drones arranged themselves into a hovering diamond above the cowering group. A cold shiver filtered through the Nagalons.

"I'm only going to say this once, so listen well," Fisher declared. "All shifters must line up, single file, and march up to the bridge. You'll be processed at the Nu Co. facility."

"They built a new facility?" said Lucy.

"Processed?" Felina swallowed.

Mrs Stricks snorted. "We're not signing up to be your next science project, Fisher."

"Not without a fight," said Chelon.

Lucy tensed. The last time the Nagalons had refused to comply with Fisher's forces, things had spun out of control, fast.

"I have a better idea, Richard," said the Other Mrs Stricks. "Why don't you take your toy soldiers home and make yourself a nice cup of cocoa." Her eyes flashed with a swirling crimson light, like a pair of dazzling roses. A loud clap of thunder sounded as her power drew a gathering of thick clouds overhead.

Fisher smirked. "Thanks for the suggestion, but I don't have much of a sweet tooth." Quick as a whip, he swung his fist up in the air.

BANG BANG BANG BANG BANG! Shots rang out faster than Lucy could count them as Fisher's commandos shot a barrage of Nu Co.-formulated darts at the shapeshifters, who scattered in every direction.

Millepoids was hit in the side by a dart filled with a neon-blue substance. He doubled over, convulsing. Lucy had previously seen what Nu Co. Blue could do to a Nagalon, but that didn't lessen her terror as Millepoids' skin bubbled and the man began to morph uncontrollably. His face sprouted whiskers and fur that rapidly changed colour from white to grey to orange. Panting as he desperately tried to regain control of his faculties, he looked up to the heavens, his eyes blazing violet.

As he did so, the empty lake basin lit up like a lava lamp and the blob illuminated in kind, its dark exterior churning with pulsing ribbons of purple light. The earth began to rumble.

It's the blob, Lucy realised. *The Nagalons use*

their powers to connect with the blob. That's what makes the ground shake!

Fisher and his men stumbled atop the quaking bridge. "Hold steady," he bellowed into his megaphone.

Carlos Felina sprinted towards the lake in a panic. FTOK! FTOK! A thick-necked goon shot the handsome weatherman in the back with two darts, each filled with the paralysing Nu Co. Pink substance. Felina howled as he froze and toppled to the ground. No longer able to move or change form at will, his face slammed into the dirt with a THUD.

Another blue dart flew past Lucy's shoulder and pierced Mrs Stricks in the bicep. The slight woman stumbled and began to morph, her arms mutating into giant wings and her neck and nose lengthening like those of an eerie flamingo. Marietta and Kenzo rushed to help her, only to find themselves petrified by pink darts.

Having grown a giant green tortoise shell, Alastair Chelon plodded slowly towards the embankment below the ring road. Darts bounced off his back and breast plates, scattering uselessly at his feet. Successfully shielding himself from the onslaught, he started to manoeuvre his heavy carapace up the hillside, but – FTOK! FTOK! FTOK! Three Pink-toting Nu Co. mercenaries struck him in the legs. Chelon stumbled, falling on to his back like a stranded whale.

Lucy watched helplessly from the beach as each of the Nagalons was taken down like wheat in the path of a harvester. But the Other Mrs Stricks was still standing in the midst of the melee, her flesh armoured with grey alligator scales, her eyes ablaze. *The shapeshifters aren't finished yet.*

"Not today, Fisher," the old woman growled. She splayed her hands at her sides, sending jagged bolts of energy into the ground. The gleam within the lake basin intensified, casting a mauve radiance across the hazy landscape.

A split second later, with a deep thrum that made Lucy's ears pop, a white pulse erupted from the blob-filled crater that washed over the chaotic lakeside like a tidal wave. Fisher's men were thrown back as the bodies of the fallen Nagalons shimmered and liquefied into large, formless balls of goo. Slowly, with a syrupy SLORRRUPP, each of the jellified aliens restored themselves to their human forms, no longer afflicted by the paralysing and hyperchanging effects of the Nu Co. substances.

Yes! Lucy looked up, hoping to see chagrin written all over Mr Fisher's face. Instead, he was an oasis of calm. Worse, he was smiling. *Oh...*

Fisher brought the bullhorn to his lips. "Playtime is over," he said, his deep voice echoing with menace. "It's time we introduced you to our newest formula. Gentlemen, deploy the drones."

In quick succession, each of the nine remote vehicles zoomed low and released plumes of thick mustard-yellow gas. The strange substance drifted down over the reinvigorated shapeshifters in sickly ropes of fog.

Lucy gagged at the saccharine stench. The Nagalons tried to run, but the Other Mrs Stricks, Scruffy Steve and Millepoids were caught in the treacly miasma. All at once, the vibrant illumination in their eyes was snuffed out, replaced by opaque wells of pitch black. The fear and anger melted from their faces. They stopped running – stopped doing anything at all – and instead stood there, staring vacantly into space.

Nu Co.'s soldiers holstered their weapons and retreated to the shadowy parts of the pathway, beyond the reach of the spotlights.

Are Fisher's goons giving up?

A memory wriggled its way out of Lucy's confused consciousness. *The bat by the billboard.* Gooseflesh rose on the back of her neck. *One of Nu Co.'s drones used yellow gas to keep it from flying away. The bat just let itself get captured, like it wasn't in control of its own mind any more.*

"Esther!" Mrs Stricks called, reaching to her wife from the sodden beachfront. "Come quickly! We must return to the Origin."

The Other Mrs Stricks looked at her partner without a flicker of recognition, inky emptiness extending across the whites of her eyes.

"Attack," Fisher commanded, his megaphoned voice ringing out across the shore.

Lucy waited for the Nu Co. security team to barrel in and capture the zombified Nagalons, but the men held their positions, standing at attention a good way away from the creatures. *Why are they ignoring their boss?* But it soon became clear that Fisher's order was not meant for his mercenaries.

In a bright blast, the Other Mrs Stricks discharged a searing web of blinding energy at Mrs Stricks, ensnaring her in place as she twisted and writhed in the mud, trying to get away.

"What are you doing?" screamed the trapped teacher.

That psycho CEO is using mind control to turn the Nagalons against one another!

A zippy drone plunged low and deposited its

sickly contents over Mrs Stricks. She opened her mouth to cry out, but no sound emerged. Instead, her features softened and her eyes went as black as unlit coals.

Scruffy Steve fired a crackling volt from beneath the archway of the bridge, narrowly missing Marietta, who was running along the track towards Mrs Stricks. The red-haired woman looked back at Steve accusingly, then turned and sprinted across the sodden beach towards the crater. Before she could get very far, Mrs Stricks stepped forth and tripped her with a quickly conjured whip of energy. No sooner had she done so when another drone zoomed past and coated Marietta in a drape of yellow mist.

Chaos reigned as the Nagalons blasted bolts at one another up and down the lakeside. From their elevated position on the bridge, Fisher, Murl and the rest of his well-dressed security squad oversaw the calamity they had sown, the electric mayhem reflecting like fireworks in their eager eyes.

Lucy bolted towards the shore. She leapt over Marietta's arms as they reached for her, then darted between Felina and Millepoids as they traded shots. Caught in the crossfire, a branching offshoot of electricity struck Lucy in the tailbone. Her insides burned as if all her organs were ablaze. Stunned, she tried to cry for help as she dropped to her knees, but all that came out was a frog-like croak.

REEAWWWKKK! The screech of a bird of prey rang out from high above. Lucy looked up to see a golden falcon descending from the starry heavens, straight towards her. She managed to raise her arm to protect herself, but the bird transformed, mid-air, into an indigo-haired boy who landed heavily beside her, tackling her into the mud.

Gus!

In a single motion, he pulled her up and into a gallop towards the open pit, away from the fighting Nagalons and Fisher's formidable men. Together they ducked and weaved across the slippery terrain as tridents of electricity flew past their heads.

"Are you OK?" he asked.

"Not really. Are you?"

Gus shook his head forlornly. "In all our time spent travelling across the universe, my people have never fought against one another. Until now."

"Until Fisher," Lucy hissed.

"And Milo." Gus yanked her down to dodge a trio of thunderbolts. "He and his father are both boughs of the same twisted tree."

"What are you talking about? What did Fish do?"

"He told his dad where to find us. I know he did."

A storm of panic churned in Lucy's chest. "No. He wouldn't do that. He promised."

Gus stopped as they neared the edge of the crater and took Lucy by the hands. "Milo doesn't trust my kind," he said, his voice quavering. "I sensed it down in the tunnel. He hates us."

ZZZZT! A jagged spark flew past them.

"You're wrong," she insisted. "Fish would never—"

BZZORTT! Gus was seized by a tangle of voltage that sent his teeth chattering wildly. Mrs Stricks had unleashed the full force of her powers upon him from twenty metres away. The boy crumpled to the ground, straining against his attacker, a line of tears staining his cheek.

"No!" Lucy flung her fist up at the men on the bridge, who were observing the madness in stony silence. "Tell them to stop. Please!"

"Lucy!" cried a voice she knew all too well.

Fish?

She turned to see Milo running towards her along the crater's steep edge.

"You have to get out of here," he shouted, waving his arms. "It's not safe for you."

"Not safe for *me*? What about the shapeshifters?" Lucy demanded. "Gus said you told your dad about the tunnel. He said you told him they were hiding down there. Is it true? Did you really betray them?"

Milo halted a few feet away, an agonised expression on his face. "It's more complicated than you think."

Lucy felt sick. "How could you?" she asked. "After Gus helped us save my dad. He brought us down there because he trusted us. He trusted *you*."

"I'm just trying to do the right thing," said Milo. "I couldn't lie to my father, not after everything he's been through."

"You lied to *me*," Lucy snarled. "I thought you were better than your dad, but it turns out you're just like him." She flung her arms out at the mustard-toned madness surrounding them. "Look at what he's done. He's controlling other people for his own profit, just like he always does. Only this time you helped him do it."

Milo hardened. "The shifters aren't people, Lucy." He focused on the blubbery abyss yawning before them. "They're the ones who've been twisting everyone's minds – you experienced it yourself! They've been manipulating you this whole time, getting you to trust them, preying on your obsession with the supernatural. But they're not like us. They're dangerous. You're just not thinking clearly."

"You're the one who's being manipulated," Lucy spat, "by your own father. He wouldn't know right from wrong if it farted in his face. And neither would you." She ducked as a drone swooped past her and engulfed the fallen Nagalon boy in a caustic cloud of yellow gas.

"Gus!" Lucy threw herself over him, but it was too late. His prone body had gone limp, his jaw slack.

"My son," Mr Fisher cried from the bridge, spotting Milo through infrared binoculars. "What is he doing here?"

"Lucy, please," said Milo. "I only wanted to protect the people I care about. I already lost my mother. I nearly lost my dad. I couldn't live with myself if I lost you too."

"Well, now you've gone and done just that," said Lucy, her voice cracking. "You're not the person I thought you were, Milo Fisher."

Hurt swimming in his eyes, Milo reached for her. "If you'd just—"

"Leave me alone!" She pulled away, backing up along the ledge. A bolt of electricity sailed past her collarbone, searing the ends of her hair.

"Milo, stay away from that pit," Fisher yelled into his megaphone. "Somebody, get my boy!"

All of the Nagalons had now been overcome by Nu Co.'s bioweaponry. SLORP, SLORP, SLORP came the sound of their footsteps as they marched across the soggy expanse towards the scuffling kids, their fingers bristling with sparks.

Behind Lucy, Gus rose from the mud, his eyes pools of nothingness. Without a word, he grabbed her by the arm and held on with a fierce grip.

"Let her go," shouted Milo. He swiped at Gus, who stumbled back a few paces, dragging Lucy closer to the cliff's edge.

"Stop," Lucy warned as she struggled to free

herself. "Gus doesn't know what he's doing. None of the shapeshifters do. They're not in control of their own actions."

"He's hurting you," said Milo. With a running start, he lunged for Gus's elbow but the Nagalon twisted out of his way, tossing Lucy painfully into the muck.

Sliding towards the precipice at a startling rate, Milo dug his feet into the mire to save himself from falling over the cliffside. He barely managed to catch his balance, breathing out a quick puff of relief when: BZZZZZZZOT! He was hit in the side by an errant bolt of energy. The force of the blast knocked him to the edge where he teetered, bewildered and dismayed, his eyes searching for something to grab on to.

Holy cripes. Fish!

Lucy leapt out to catch his hand but she swiped and missed, grasping at nothing as Milo toppled over the ledge, his mouth contorting in fear as he fell into the gaping, mile-wide hole at the centre of Sticky Pines.

No, no, no, this can't be happening.

Time slowed as down, down, down he tumbled, somersaulting head over foot, storey after storey, until – PLORRRPPPPPPPSHHH! – he landed on the gelatinous mass below.

"Milo!" Lucy's scream was joined by an even more agonised cry from Mr Fisher, who watched, horror-struck, as his only son was slurped into the shimmering surface of the blob, disappearing in an instant.

CHAPTER 18

Message Sent

High up on a hillside overlooking Black Hole Lake, under the shadow of the Big Crater Valley's tallest billboard, a large hairy creature with big sharp teeth peered down upon the wild events below.

Where had all the lake water gone? Why were all those people fighting? And what was that yellow cloud floating around them? It smelled sweet. Was it food? Were the people fighting because they were hungry? These questions and more held Errol's rapt attention.

His belly rumbled as he dropped the forked tree branch he was carrying into a pile of sticks he'd spent the evening collecting. Errol was of the opinion that you could never have enough sticks. Earlier, he'd spotted a rabbit he'd been hoping to catch, but it had gotten away. It was pretty smart for a rabbit, but it wasn't one of the ones that could change into a bird or a badger. It was just a regular old rabbit. Sometimes it was hard to tell the difference, even for Errol. Animals in Sticky Pines could be tricky like that.

The snap of a twig sent the dog's floppy ears straight up. He sniffed the air. Someone was close by.

Footsteps crunched through the underbrush behind him. It sounded like a human. A medium-sized human. One that was walking quickly towards him.

Pinning his ears back and stiffly extending his tail, Errol turned to face the intruder.

A silver-haired woman sporting corduroy trousers and a wool gilet pushed aside a low pine branch and stepped out on to the open hillside. She paused when she saw the enormous wolfhound before her.

Errol recognised the lady's scent from when his two-legged mother and sisters returned from the big red building with all the pencils in it. Though her smell was familiar, Errol wasn't sure whether he liked it. He issued a low growl from the depths of his throat and bared his mighty teeth. If nothing else, he needed to command her respect.

The woman stared quietly at the growling beast. Then her skin began to glimmer and vibrate. She shook her head rapidly, spraying clear slime in all directions as her neck and face stretched, sprouting short black hairs that extended from a long pointed snout all the way to the tall triangular ears that grew atop her head. Now a human with the head of a dog, the woman barked and snarled ferociously.

Terrified, Errol squealed and bolted away, scampering past the billboard and into the forest, heading home to his log cabin as fast as he could run.

Good dog, thought Principal Pakuna.

She strode to the edge of the ridge and surveyed the carnage unfolding on the lakeshore. Her resilient people had finally, after an eternity of peaceful coexistence, been overcome by an enemy force. She watched as they were lined up on the spotlit path like mindless automatons and then marched single-file up the embankment and on to the Borealis Bridge. There, a cluster of suited men herded them into SUVs and drove them across the arched expanse towards the Nu Co. property.

Pakuna focused on the pulsing crater before her, her breast welling with sorrow. The Origin was exposed. The mother of the Nagalons, the beating heart of their ancient civilisation, cruelly laid bare by those greedy, larval primates. Didn't the humans know that what lay at the bottom of that lake was the source of all that made Sticky Pines such an exceptional place? *Fools.* Her lip curled in anger.

The apes were gathered around the edge of

the crater, shouting and shrieking and discharging projectiles into the Origin. *Senseless desecration.* The stench of their colourful weapons made her nauseous. Nu Co.'s substances were nothing but a toxic perversion of the majestic life force flowing beneath the Big Crater Valley. Nucralose, that miraculous material, had been polluted by inferior human chemicals and used to ambush and imprison the members of her benevolent species.

Living among the humans has brought nothing but centuries and centuries of barbaric madness. It was time for a critical decision to be made. Pakuna had never considered that she needed to be the one to make it, but there was no one else left to do so. *We must act decisively. There's not a moment to waste.*

With a certainty of purpose, Pakuna marched back towards the billboard. She could have morphed into a bird and flown up to the wooden platform, but she rather appreciated her current hybrid form. Her canine head reminded her of one of humanity's ancient gods, who judged the deeds of mankind before ushering them into the afterlife. *How appropriate.*

She leapt up and grabbed the first rung of the billboard's ladder. One-handed, she pulled up her slight frame with easy strength and climbed to the top. The frantic shouts at the lakeside grew louder as she ascended to her perch.

When she reached the summit, Pakuna glanced scathingly at the oversized smiling clown before turning her cool gaze upon the landscape. Even under the glint of a half moon, Sticky Pines was astonishing to behold. The forest spread out across the dale like a blanket of soft, knobbly wool. The starry sky was dotted with sporadic clouds that floated like weightless ships across an endless sea. *It's such a shame.* Pakuna clucked her tongue. *This planet was a uniquely beautiful habitat.*

Her hip brushed against something odd attached to the guard rail beside her: some sort of metal canister no bigger than a football, with a small satellite dish affixed to it. The alien principal adjusted her pupils for better night vision. On the side of the contraption was a piece of duct tape, with the words "Property of Lucy Sladan" written in indelible ink. *Hmph. So this is how that girl spends her time instead of completing her assigned reading.*

Pakuna turned back to face the colossal crater. *Don't worry, my kindred. Soon we will be free of this cruel world.* She held out her hands and opened her palms towards the heavens, reaching out to the Origin with her mind. Her irises shone orange, then red, then violet. In the distance, the entity at the base of the waterless lake illuminated in turn.

Sparks danced between her fingers as every hair on her canine snout quivered. The ground trembled softly, causing the billboard to sway. Lucy's satellite device began to emit a low, persistent beeping noise. Ignoring it, Pakuna lifted her arms above her head, channelling a stream of bright-white energy between her palms. The billboard lights flickered.

It's time to call for backup.

Looking inward, Pakuna concentrated on composing a message. The light bulbs behind her shattered in a rain of incandescence as the Origin used its power to dissipate the clouds, clearing the skies above the Big Crater Valley. The opalescent blob began to churn in a luminous vortex, creating a sunken opening in its domed centre.

Casting her arms forward, Pakuna expelled a shaft of energy from her hands. It shot across the drained lake like a laser and descended into the spinning hole. The Origin glowed brighter, pulsating with purpose, then shot a brief but fierce jet of light into the sky, through the atmosphere, out of the solar system and straight towards a galaxy far, far beyond.

Lucy's extraterrestrial dispatch detector beeped like mad.

Pakuna leaned against the railing, much of her strength spent. A warm sensation at her back alerted her to the fact that the billboard was now on fire. *Whoops.* But it was worth it. The Nagalons' final distress signal had been sent to a fierce alien ally:

Transmission URGENT: the Nagalons are in mortal danger. The Pretenders have succeeded in overcoming our defences. The Origin is exposed. The time has come to evacuate Earth. We are in need of immediate assistance. SEND THE ADMINISTERS OF INTERGALACTIC REDRESS. End transmission.

Straightening her weary back, Pakuna regarded the panicked Earthlings below, scrabbling about like a deranged colony of termites as the blob dimmed and sealed the opening at its centre. She could only hope that the help she'd requested would arrive in time. Mr Fisher was a treacherous beast. He'd captured her people and was surely intent on their destruction. It wouldn't be long before he found a way to harm the Origin too. For now, fortunately, the sacred entity was capable of protecting itself.

Pakuna hopped atop the railing, balancing precariously on the arches of her feet. A warm breeze ruffled the fur on her ears. With a deep breath, she jumped. Shuddering in mid-air, she transformed into a blackbird and flew up, up, up into the night sky, her silhouette a tiny, fluttering dot against a silvery moon that hung sombrely above the sleepy timber rooftops of Sticky Pines. All the while, the message she had sent was travelling at millions of miles per second, fast approaching its fateful destination.

ACKNOWLEDGEMENTS

Thank you to everyone who has undertaken this twisty and exciting journey with me, especially all the lovely people who have offered support and assistance along the way. And my undying thanks to Sticky Pineseans all over the world, who have helped make writing these books more fun than I could have possibly imagined.

THiS WEiRD WORLD

Dear Reader,

People have often asked me where the idea for the Sticky Pines series came from. To put it simply, the inspiration for these books was drawn from the world around us, which, I now understand, is far weirder than I had imagined.

When I first started writing these books, I, like many authors, looked to the familiar for inspiration. But what's most surprised me is just how much I've been inspired by what I *don't* know. The protagonist of Sticky Pines, Lucy Sladan, is a girl who believes in the Unknown and is desperate to change the world by being the first to uncover something truly extraordinary. She's certain that there are things out there – strange, supernatural, cryptozoological things that defy common sense and understanding – just waiting to be discovered. In the books, Lucy starts out almost entirely alone in this belief, but I, for one, now realise that she's really on to something!

As Lucy finds out throughout the Sticky Pines saga, what the human race doesn't know or has forgotten about life on Earth could fill more books than have ever been written. This was something I found quite surprising. I was raised at a time when the prevailing sentiment seemed to be that humans already knew everything worth knowing. We had medicine and computers and refrigerators and physics and e-books and cars and styrofoam and chicken nuggets and cable TV.

As a kid growing up in 1990s America, the general feeling seemed to be that we had reached the end of history. We'd cracked the code of existence! Nothing big would change ever again! What else was there to do but pat ourselves on the back and wait for Utopia to take effect.

And then came THE INTERNET. All of humanity's common knowledge was laid out on the World Wide Web, available at the press of a few buttons, for free! It was the Age of Information and, boy, what a lot of information there was. It seemed that the breadth of our wisdom was infinite. How could there possibly be anything left to be discovered? And yet…

They say the more you know, the more you realise you don't know. (Who are "They"? I don't know!) In conducting research for the series, I quickly learned just how ignorant I was about how much of the world, let alone the universe, is still beyond human understanding. For example, there have been incredible advancements in the field of medicine over the last couple of centuries – we've discovered DNA and psychology, we've created bionic limbs and treatments for cancer – and yet we still don't know some pretty basic things. Like, why do animals need to sleep?

Every single person, elephant and hummingbird who's ever lived has fallen unconscious for a significant portion of every single day. Sleep is one of the most essential parts of being alive, but though scientists are discovering new things about sleep all the time, we still don't know precisely why people need to do it, and what exactly is happening in the brain when we do. What are dreams? Do they mean anything or are they just random bursts of electricity? Do sharks dream? Do trees? We don't know!

There is so much to learn about the natural world that people are still discovering new things about it every single day. Have you ever heard of the mimic octopus? It's a cephalopod that can change its shape, texture and colouring to match anything from jagged purple rocks to black-and-white striped sea snakes to flamboyant lionfish. How about the decoy spider, a tiny arachnid which builds a big spider suit in its web out of leaf bits and other debris to scare off predators? It plucks at strands of silk to make its giant disguise look like it's moving, a disguise which, I might add, often has exactly eight legs. That's right. Spiders can count. Who knew?

History is filled with examples of humans believing they knew all there was to be known, and then being rudely disabused of this presumption. From declaring that the Earth was at the centre of our celestial sphere, to the belief that diseases were caused by evil spirits, to the misconception that tigers, giant squid and whales were merely the stuff of legend, it turns out that humans are routinely getting it wrong. It takes remarkable people, those who are brave enough to be called crazy by the rest of society, to break through the veneer of misplaced certainty. People like Lucy Sladan.

Lucy believes that something is Out There, something she doesn't fully understand, and she endures a great deal in order to prove to the world that she's right. It's been a delight taking this journey with her, and each time I sit down to write another volume of the Sticky Pines saga, I enjoy being surprised, again and again, at just how inspiring this weird world can be.

Your friend,
Dashe Roberts